OVERDUE WISHES

THE WISHING TREE SERIES, BOOK 10

TAMMY L. GRACE

PRAISE FOR TAMMY L. GRACE

"I had planned on an early night but couldn't put this book down until I finished it around 3am. Like her other books, this one features fascinating characters with a plot that mimics real life in the best way. My recommendation: it's time to read every book Tammy L Grace has written."
— *Carolyn, review of Beach Haven*

"This book is a clean, simple romance with a background story very similar to the works of Debbie Macomber. If you like Macomber's books you will like this one. A holiday tale filled with dogs, holiday fun, and the joy of giving will warm your heart.
— *Avid Mystery Reader, review of A Season for Hope: A Christmas Novella*

"This book was just as enchanting as the others.

Hardships with the love of a special group of friends. I recommend the series as a must read. I loved every exciting moment. A new author for me. She's fabulous."
—*Maggie! review of Pieces of Home: A Hometown Harbor Novel (Book 4)*

"Tammy is an amazing author, she reminds me of Debbie Macomber… Delightful, heartwarming…just down to earth."
— *Plee, review of A Promise of Home: A Hometown Harbor Novel (Book 3)*

"This was an entertaining and relaxing novel. Tammy Grace has a simple yet compelling way of drawing the reader into the lives of her characters. It was a pleasure to read a story that didn't rely on theatrical tricks, unrealistic events or steamy sex scenes to fill up the pages. Her characters and plot were strong enough to hold the reader's interest."
—*MrsQ125, review of Finding Home: A Hometown Harbor Novel (Book 1)*

"This is a beautifully written story of loss, grief, forgiveness and healing. I believe anyone could relate to the situations and feelings represented here. This is a read that will stay with you long after you've completed the book."
—*Cassidy Hop, review of Finally Home: A Hometown Harbor Novel (Book 5)*

"Killer Music is a clever and well-crafted whodunit. The vivid and colorful characters shine as the author gradually reveals their hidden secrets—an absorbing page-turning read."
— *Jason Deas, bestselling author of Pushed and Birdsongs*

"I could not put this book down! It was so well written & a suspenseful read! This is definitely a 5-star story! I'm hoping there will be a sequel!"
—*Colleen, review of Killer Music*

"This is the best book yet by this author. The plot was well crafted with an unanticipated ending. I like to try to leap ahead and see if I can accurately guess the outcome. I was able to predict some of the plot but not the actual details which made reading the last several chapters quite engrossing."

—*0001PW, review of Deadly Connection*

Overdue Wishes
The Wishing Tree Series, Book 10

The Wishing Tree SERIES

Tammy L. Grace

Overdue Wishes
By
Tammy L. Grace

OVERDUE WISHES is a work of fiction. Names, characters, places and incidents either are products of the author's imagination or are used fictitiously. Any resemblance to actual events, locales, entities, or persons, living or dead, is entirely coincidental.

www.tammylgrace.com
Published in the United States by Lone Mountain Press, Nevada
Printed in the United States of America
ISBN 978-1-945591-35-8 (paperback)
ISBN 978-1-945591-31-0 (eBook)
FIRST EDITION
Cover by Elizabeth Mackey Graphic Design

For our wonderful readers in My Book Friends

ALSO BY TAMMY L. GRACE

Hometown Harbor: The Beginning

Finding Home

Home Blooms

A Promise of Home

Pieces of Home

Finally Home

Forever Home

Killer Music

Deadly Connection

Dead Wrong

Cold Killer

A Season for Hope

The Magic of the Season

Christmas in Snow Valley

One Unforgettable Christmas

Christmas Sisters

Christmas Wishes

Christmas Surprises

Christmas Shelter

Beach Haven

Moonlight Beach

Beach Dreams

The Wishing Tree

Wish Again

Overdue Wishes

WRITING AS CASEY WILSON

A Dog's Hope
A Dog's Chance

CHAPTER 1

*N*orma finally plopped down in the chair behind the registration table, satisfied her prep work was done. She and the other volunteers had worked so hard over the last few months to pull together the Linden Falls All-Class Reunion. A born organizer, Norma had taken on the bulk of the behind-the-scenes work, and now, seeing all the white tents set up in the town square, she could relax and enjoy the fruits of her labor.

The committee had settled on late August for the celebration, with the hopes of avoiding the street-clogging crowds that came in September when the foliage was often at its peak in color. They weren't sure what to expect as far as numbers, but they all knew with the celebration of Linden Falls' two hundred fiftieth birthday, it was the perfect excuse for such an event.

Norma adjusted the front of her cardigan sweater over her green and gold school shirt with the huge

1

falcon on the front of it. Her athletic hopes were long gone, but it was a day to show her school spirit and support the Linden Falls Falcons. The sun was rising into the flawless blue sky, and with all the running around, the slight chill in the air didn't faze her. In fact, if it got much warmer, she'd have to ditch her sweater.

She straightened the stack of name tags and pens on the table and took a sip from her water bottle. The weather promised to be in the mid-seventies, with no rain in the forecast. They couldn't ask for more than that. From her perch under the registration tent, Norma enjoyed the view of the beautiful Wishing Tree, her full branches loaded down with wishes. Neva was on the committee and suggested they leave as many wishes as they could, weather permitting, since it encouraged visitors to add their own wishes to the branches.

Neva had been out early while the town workers were setting up to make sure the wooden box at the base of the tree was stocked with plenty of paper and ribbons. She'd also brought Norma a lovely cup of tea, infused with some of Janie's special honey. She glanced at the empty mug next to her and picked it up, walking across the square to Neva's. She could use a refill.

Neva was looking especially beautiful today, with a lovely scarf in pale pink draped around her neck. Her eyes lit up when she noticed the empty mug. "Shall I refill that for you, Norma?"

Norma smiled and handed it to her. "It was delicious."

"That was Janie's cinnamon and vanilla. It's perfect for the upcoming fall season, don't you think?"

"I need to buy some. Can you save me a jar?"

"Of course. I'll set one aside for you." She handed her the steaming mug. "The square looks lovely. You've done such a great job putting all this together. I've got a full house staying here this weekend. Every room in a fifty-mile radius is booked. The chamber of commerce should give you an award."

Norma's cheeks colored and she grinned. "That's great news. I'm looking forward to seeing old students. Even though I didn't grow up here and attend school, thirty years at the high school library makes me feel like I know just about every person in town, and their parents." They both laughed.

"When you've lived as long as we have, it does seem that way." Neva looked out the window at her beloved tree. "Sometimes, I feel like I'm as old as our tree. Imagine what she's seen in her lifetime. It's fascinating to think of the history and people who have passed by her. All the changes and she's still the same graceful lady." Neva's eyes twinkled and it seemed like she was far away as she gazed upon it.

She turned her attention away from the tree and back to Norma. "Have you attended your high school reunions? I'm not sure I even know where you went to high school."

Norma brushed the question aside and pointed to the square. "I better get back to my post." Norma turned to leave and Neva hurried to grab a paper bag from behind her. "I packed up a few maple scones for you. You might not have time for a break."

"Thank you. That's so kind of you." She peeked inside the bag and breathed in the delicious aroma. "I don't think I'll be waiting long to sample one." She waved goodbye and hurried back to the registration tables.

Soon, volunteers began to arrive and Norma went over the folders she had prepared and the clipboards where returning students could sign their name and provide their contact information. If the event went over well, the mayor wanted to do it every year.

Norma made sure the volunteers saw the stack of maps, which highlighted each of the class tents that were positioned around the square, making it easy for classmates to find their class to gather and visit. "The concert starts at seven o'clock and we have a few food trucks coming in this afternoon."

After she got the volunteers situated at the tables, organized by year of graduation, Norma dug out a scone and nibbled at it while she sipped her tea. She closed her eyes, enjoying the fall flavors that mingled in her mouth. Her favorite season was just around the corner and she couldn't wait to bake up some pumpkin muffins that would go great with the new honey.

The Winey Widows had volunteered to help cover the registration tables but wouldn't be putting in their shifts until later in the day. Norma had arrived at the square with the sunrise to supervise the setup and place all the signage around the square and surrounding blocks. She cherished the relative peace and quiet of the early morning and, while she could have scheduled someone to help her, enjoyed the solitude.

With Margot gone, Norma was the only early riser among them. She longed for their early-morning visits on Margot's porch, both of them sipping hot tea and solving the world's problems together. Well, maybe not the world's, but at least those of Linden Falls—their world.

She missed Margot but loved watching Paige flourish in her new role as the proprietor of Town Square Books. All of the Winey Widows had been so worried about Paige, but with the arrival of Reed and their old connection rekindled, she had begun to thrive again. After they were married, he'd moved into the house with Paige and Gladys and spent a lot of his time upstairs writing his novels but always made time to join Paige for lunch. He quit writing in the midafternoon and had taken to cooking all their evening meals.

Margot would have been thrilled to see her sweet girl smiling again. She would be so happy to see Paige cherished and with a man like Reed, who was so obviously devoted to her. It would have warmed her heart to know Paige was getting back to her art and was dipping her toe back into illustrating books. Sometimes, as Norma knew all too well, life was unfair.

As the hours went by and it was almost noon, the square was filled with people, laughing and visiting, reminiscing and excited to see friends they hadn't seen in years. Norma fielded questions and pointed out things to see and do, highlighting several tours of historic buildings in the town, including the schools, and the hike to Linden Falls, not too far out of town. The town hadn't changed all that much in the last several decades, but along with cherished memories, there were new shops and businesses, new restaurants, and even a new distillery with popular tastings.

Norma's height gave her an advantage and she could see over the top of most of the crowd. She spotted Constable Pike handing out plastic badges to a group of children, working hard to build their trust that law enforcement was their friend.

Doc's was the most popular gathering place, with most of the prior students remembering it from their time growing up in Linden Falls. The sidewalk outside was crowded with people sipping drinks and running into old friends, trying to remember names and connections.

Everywhere Norma looked, people were smiling and hugging one another. It was all she had imagined when she had come up with the idea. She wasn't much for the spotlight and preferred to let the mayor's office take all the credit for the event but enjoyed the challenge of organizing it and making it all work.

Paige popped by Norma's table just before noon and set a plate down in front of her. She pointed across the square. "That food truck has the best breakfast sandwiches. I thought you might be getting hungry, so I nabbed one."

Norma eyed the thick roll, loaded with eggs and bacon and oozing melted cheese. "That looks so good and I shouldn't even be hungry. Neva treated me to one of her scones."

Paige smiled. "Calories don't count today. I think you've earned it." She glanced around the square. "You've got a great turnout. We've been hopping at the bookstore. I'd say it's quite the success."

Norma nodded and smiled as she took in everyone milling about, lawn chairs covering the grassy area. "I'm just happy everyone is enjoying themselves. You and Reed be sure and come over for the concert tonight."

"We wouldn't miss it. If you need anything between now and then, just give me a buzz. If you get a dinner break, maybe you can join us. Reed is packing us a picnic supper."

"That sounds lovely. I think I will have eaten more today than I have all week."

Paige turned and waved as she jogged back to the store.

Norma finished the yummy sandwich and relieved one of the other volunteers so she could get some lunch. Over the next few hours, Norma visited with many former students she remembered. When they saw her name tag, most of them would point and holler out that they remembered her. Mrs. Braxton, the librarian.

She didn't mind that her occupation defined her. She loved books. They had been her best friends and she loved being surrounded by them, helping students do their research projects, long before online search engines. Her greatest satisfaction came from introducing students who didn't share her love of reading to a book she knew would be perfect for them. She had changed many nonreaders into students who became regulars, gobbling up series of books she would recommend. She was a book whisperer long before the phrase had been coined.

Norma had devoured books in college and continued that practice throughout her adult life. Being a librarian had afforded her the luxury of being paid to read. Students would often ask her how many books she had read. She would always just smile and tell them more than they could imagine.

She couldn't bring herself to share that she actually kept track. She had a leather journal she stored in her desk where she recorded each book she read. One book per line, in her precise cursive handwriting. Title, author, and her own star rating system were included on each line. She kicked herself for not putting the date. Instead, she simply noted each year at the top of the page. Her first entry had been more than forty-five years ago.

By the time she retired, she had recorded over six thousand books in her journals. Those were just the books she read at work. She had several other journals at home. She had longed to organize them and often thought about transferring all the information to a computer so she could sort it by author and title, but there was something comforting, almost soothing, to holding the worn leather in her hands and perusing the handwritten pages. Inks had faded over time, but they were all readable.

If anyone knew how many total books she had read, they would be shocked. They either wouldn't believe her or think she was nuts. Never having had children, she had filled her time off with reading. It had always been her escape, her refuge. When Bob had passed away, she turned to her books even more. Her long-time friend, Cecilia, from the grief group, and now the Winey Widows had helped her discover a world beyond the pages of her books, but they'd always be part of her life.

Bob had worked hard but didn't make much money as an appliance repairman and didn't get much time off, so their vacations had been limited. When he'd passed away, Norma received his life insurance money and had made some smart investments with it that, together with her pension, made for a comfortable life and one in which she could afford to take a few trips with her friends.

She lived a simple life, quite happy in her small cottage, the same one she and Bob had lived in since they were married. It had everything she needed, plus the bookcases Bob had made for her that housed all her favorites. Her books and her knitting in the winter, along with her flower garden in the warmer months, provided all the entertainment she needed. By keeping her living expenses low, she could splurge on travel with the Winey Widows, always looking forward to their next adventure. That was key, she had discovered. Having something fun planned gave her a purpose.

The all-class reunion had given her a focus and purpose this past year. She'd had such fun planning it, looking through all the old yearbooks, searching online and social media to find students from earlier decades who had moved away from Linden Falls. She let out a long breath as she took in the square, completely filled with classmates. It brought her immense satisfaction.

Her musings were interrupted when two men approached her table. Her eyes were drawn to the taller of the two, perhaps because he had a noticeable limp. They both smiled at her and the shorter one said, "I need to register. Class of 1966. Joe Freeman."

Norma flipped to his name and checked him off her list, handing him a clipboard. "We're so glad you're here. Your class tent is right over there." She pointed to a row closest to Main Street.

He glanced back at the taller man. "I talked my friend into coming along with me. He's in the band that's playing tonight. He's their drummer." He grinned at Norma. "Come on up here, Chet."

The tall man grinned, exposing the dimples framing his silver-streaked mustache that drifted into an even grayer patch of beard on his chin. She glanced up to his stunning blue eyes, behind the round tortoiseshell glasses he wore, and stifled a gasp. Her lips almost whispered his name, but she pressed them together before it could escape.

CHAPTER 2

"*D*o I need to register?" Chet asked in a gravelly voice.

She swallowed hard and said, "It's up to you. I have a clipboard here for guests." She slid it across the table.

His forehead creased as he looked at her and then at the white name tag attached to her sweater. "Norma. It is Norma. I thought it was you. Norma Lenox, right?"

She blinked a few times and glanced down at her paperwork. "No, I'm Norma Braxton."

He filled out his name on the clipboard and shook his head. "But your maiden name was Lenox, right? You lived in Stockbridge."

She took the clipboard back from him. "Sorry, I think you've got me confused with someone else."

He grinned again, exposing those dimples she would recognize anywhere, even if it had been over fifty years. "Sorry, I could swear…"

A woman wandered up and put her arm around

Joe's shoulders. "Joe, I can't believe you came. She hugged him and pressed her lips to his cheek.

He smiled from ear to ear. "Susie, I'd know you anywhere. You haven't aged at all." He turned toward Chet. "I want you to meet my good friend Chet. He's in the band that will be playing later tonight."

Two more people stepped behind the three of them and Norma craned her neck to the side, motioning the two newcomers forward, hoping the others would move along. As the couple stepped forward, it forced Joe and Susie to move farther away and Chet followed, but not before he looked at Norma one more time. "You have a nice evening, Norma."

She nodded. "Same to you. Enjoy yourself." She quickly turned her attention to the new registrants and took an extra-long time explaining all the events, willing Chet and Joe to get lost in the crowd.

As soon as she finished talking, the couple left in search of their class tent. Norma peeled off her cardigan and made a new name tag for herself. She finished writing and stuck it to her T-shirt. *Mrs. Braxton.* She sighed and told the woman next to her she needed a quick break.

Norma hurried across the street to Town Square Books. Paige had told her she was welcome to use the facilities throughout the day, since Norma wasn't a fan of the portable toilets the town had brought in for the event. Paige was getting ready to close but looked up from the register as Norma came through the door.

"Are you okay?" she asked. "Your face is bright red."

Norma waved her hand in front of her face. "I just got a bit overheated. I should have taken my sweater off hours ago. I'll just be a minute. I don't want to keep you from closing."

She ducked into the restroom and ran cool water over her wrists. It was something her grandmother had always recommended if Norma was feeling warm or had a fever. She looked in the mirror above the sink, taking in her lackluster hair that was more mousy looking than the stylish silver gray that so many ladies her age were sporting. Maybe if it was made up of beautiful shades of silver and gray, she could embrace it more happily, like Neva had. She wore no makeup or jewelry and her clothes hung on her thin frame. At least her skin, not as taut as it used to be, was clear and free of wrinkles. Tears filled her eyes. She was just so… so beige. Her sweater, her skin, her hair. Her entire life. It all was one big colorless blob.

Her relative obscurity and beige-ness had served her well. Usually, nobody gave her a second glance. It had camouflaged her and let her become unremarkable. She was the typical quiet librarian with her nose always in a book, hiding away with her beloved stacks of them.

She let the cool water soothe her and wiped her face with a damp paper towel.

Pull yourself together, Norma.

Chet wouldn't be here long. She just needed to avoid him, which should be easy with him taking the stage with the band. She'd be able to keep her eye on him. She'd overheard Joe mention he was leaving in the morning, so she just had to get through tonight.

She hadn't left Stockbridge all those years ago and made a new life to have it all come crashing down now. Images of the past flashed in her mind. She hadn't thought about her youth, Stockbridge, or Chet in decades. Not even Bob had known the truth.

Why now? Why did she feel like everything was about to unravel? All her carefully constructed work would be for nothing. If her friends found out, what would she do? She was too old to pack up and move.

Her heart began pounding in her ears as she contemplated the worst-case scenario. She had a bad habit of going full-on pessimist. She had to shake it off and get back out there. She'd stay busy, and if the band took a break, she'd make sure she was lost in the crowd. She had planned to stay until the evening was over, but she could pack up the registration tables and go home early, before the concert ended. That would guarantee she wouldn't accidentally bump into Chet again.

A soft tapping on the door startled her. "Norma, are you okay?" Paige's voice was quiet but filled with concern.

"Oh, yes, dear. I'm fine. I was just trying to cool off." She removed the damp towel she had placed on the back of her neck. Another trick from her grandma. She longed for those early days when she hadn't had a care in the world and would listen to her grandma read her stories. Norma had loved to cuddle next to her and breathe in the rose scent that always followed her.

She wiped the counter and tossed her damp towels in the trash and opened the door. Paige was standing on the other side, her brow furrowed. "Are you sure you're okay? I can take over the table if you need to rest."

Norma waved her away. Disappearing now would just create more of a stir and bring unnecessary attention to her. That was the last thing she needed. "I'm feeling much better. Just a bit overheated."

Paige tilted her head and Gladys stepped forward and leaned against Norma's leg. "You have to promise to call me if you feel worse."

Norma smiled and reached for Paige's arm. "You're such a sweet girl, Paige. Thank you, but I'll be fine. It's just been a long day."

She bent down and gave Gladys a good scratch behind her ears. Norma never had dogs and wasn't a huge fan of them but over the years had warmed to Gladys and considered her a friend.

She took a deep breath and waved goodbye to Paige as she headed out the door and back to the square. She was stopped several times on her way to the registration table. Students she remembered reached out to hug her and ask her how she was doing while telling her about their lives.

By the time she returned to her chair, it was almost time for the band to begin. The mayor had taken the stage and was thanking everyone for being there, touting the perfect weather, as if he had arranged it. Norma smirked, and then when she heard him announce her name, her heart fell, and dread lurched in her stomach.

He looked around, asking where Norma was, her name blasted over the speaker system loud and clear. There was no escape. He wanted her on the stage. If she didn't go, it would be worse. The band was already set up and Chet was sitting behind his drums, dead center, right behind where the mayor was standing.

She was on the far end of the square and had to walk through throngs of people, all of them clapping and smiling for her, showering her with accolades. It was the longest walk of her life, and with each step she took, it was like sinking deeper into quicksand.

The crowd roared with applause as she climbed the steps to the stairs and stood next to Mayor O'Brien. He was trying to be nice and acknowledge all of Norma's work, but she had told him she didn't want any recognition. He presented her with a huge bouquet of flowers and an engraved plaque. Norma thanked him and scurried from the microphone before he could ask her to say anything.

As she rushed away, she felt Chet's eyes on her and couldn't help herself. She turned back to look at him. He winked and she made tracks for the safety of her registration table.

As she was making her way back, the band began to play. Despite their goofy name, the Rockin' Chairs, they were actually quite good. The crowd was already loving it, bouncing and swaying to the rhythm of a popular song from the 1960s.

Norma's fifteen minutes of fame was soon forgotten. Everyone was too busy enjoying the music, chatting, and making visits to the old silver Airstream trailer that doubled as a mobile bar. The band were thirty minutes into their ninety-minute performance when Norma made the decision to let the registration volunteers go. There hadn't been many new people arriving and she wanted to clean up and get home before the band decided to take a break.

She gathered all the binders and clipboards and stored them in the plastic totes stacked at the back of their tent. Reed and Paige were seated close to the table and, when they saw Norma working, jumped to their feet to help her.

Reed carried all the totes across the street to Norma's car, parked on the side of the bookstore. She left one clipboard and a few name tags out and Paige promised to keep an eye on them and help anyone who showed up after Norma left.

Paige pointed to the bookstore. "Norma, if you'd like to listen to the music, you're welcome to go inside the house or sit out on the porch. It's a shame you did all this work and are missing out on most of the concert."

Norma smiled but waved off her offer. "Thank you, Paige. I think I've just put in too many hours today. I'm spent from all the work and excitement. Besides, I bet I can still hear the music from my place."

Paige laughed. "You're probably right. I sometimes forget how small Linden Falls really is. You have a great night and get some rest tomorrow."

Paige and Reed waited on the sidewalk as Norma backed her small SUV out of their side driveway. She waved to them and headed away from the town square, sad to miss out on the rest of the evening but relieved to put some distance between her and Chet.

SUNDAY MORNING, Norma slept soundly and didn't wake until almost seven o'clock. She chastised herself for oversleeping but figured her body needed the extra rest. Feeling less vulnerable and more like her old self, Norma filled the kettle and brewed a cup of her favorite Earl Grey tea. She wished she had taken the time to go to Neva's and pick up that jar of honey.

After her tea and a shower, she put on her walking shoes and headed out for her morning constitutional, albeit several hours later than usual. She tucked her wallet in her pocket, intent on stopping at Neva's to get her honey. It was another lovely morning and Linden Falls was looking crisp and bright, bathed in sunlight. As she took the turn to Main Street and crossed over by Town Square Books, she noticed the town workers were in the square taking down the tents and packing up the tables and chairs they had stationed at the registration area.

The stage was empty, and they were taking it apart

to store it in the big barn where they kept all the town's holiday decorations and various things they used at special events. Soon, the town square would be back to normal and the only evidence of the hundreds of people that had been there last night would be the extra wishes hanging in the branches of the Wishing Tree.

Neva had been in her element, explaining the legend of the tree to anyone who didn't know it, encouraging them to add a wish while they were there. She had filled the box with purple ribbons yesterday and Norma noticed lots of purple strings hanging in the tree this morning. Neva's enchanting tales about her beloved tree were powerful and convincing, and everyone who lived in Linden Falls knew they'd be wise not to underestimate her persuasive charms.

It was after eleven when Norma made her way to Neva's door. The breakfast part of her service would be over, so she wouldn't be interrupting her at a busy time. As she opened the door, a golden retriever bounded out of it and right into her. "Gladys, is that you? You silly girl."

A deep voice from around the corner said, "No, I'm afraid this is Willy, but I bet he'd love to meet Gladys."

Chet stepped into view. "Morning, Norma. Nice to see you."

Norma struggled for words as Willy's tail slapped against her legs. Seriously, Chet Nelson had named his dog Willy? She stifled a laugh and the urge to comment

19

on it. "Good morning to you. I'm surprised you're still here."

"Well, I decided to stick around a bit. There's something special about this little town and I've got nowhere to be. Joe took off this morning, back to Boston."

"Oh...well, uh, I hope you enjoy your stay."

Neva drifted in from wherever she had been and handed Norma the jar of honey. "I see you've met my newest guest, Chet."

Norma took hold of the honey, gripping it like it was lemon she was trying to squeeze. "Oh, yes, we met last night."

Neva's eyes sparkled with mischief. "He's quite the drummer, isn't he?" The phone rang and Neva left to answer it.

Norma nodded. "I don't know much about music but enjoyed it, and the crowd loved the band."

Chet stepped closer to Norma. "You didn't even stick around until the end. I went to look for you when we finished up and the lady that owns the bookstore told me you'd gone home."

Norma nodded. "Yes, I'd worked all day and ducked out a bit early."

"Let me treat you to brunch or breakfast or whatever you want. I was just heading out myself. Neva recommended the Crooked Porch."

Norma shook her head. "Oh, no. I've got things to do. You enjoy it though."

"You're sure I can't persuade you?" Chet asked.

His dimples made it hard to resist, but she stuck to her guns. "No, but thank you." Her hands began to sweat and made the jar slick. It fell from her hands and luckily landed on a thick rug Neva had placed over the hardwood flooring.

She bent to pick it up, feeling the blood rush to her cheeks and hearing her heart pounding in her ears, but before she could get it, Chet plucked it from the rug.

He brought it up close to his face and scrutinized it, then held it up in front of the window to inspect it. "I think it's good. I don't see any cracks."

He placed it in Norma's outstretched hand. "Are you okay? You look a little flushed."

"I'm fine. Thank you." She took the honey and hurried out the front door before he could ask her any more questions.

As she made her way around the square, taking care not to go near the Crooked Porch, she stopped after she passed by Paige's place. She gritted her teeth and looked down at the honey jar in her hand. "After all that, I can't believe I forgot to pay Neva."

She turned around and walked back to the Wishing Tree Inn. She risked a peek through the door and there was no sign of Chet or his dog. Neva greeted her as she came through the door. "I've just brewed a pot of tea and taken out some blackberry scones. Join me, won't you?"

Somehow, Neva always knew what people needed. Apparently, Norma needed a warm blackberry scone, a cup of tea, and a bit of a visit. She sat at one of Neva's antique tables and sniffed at the single pink rose in the vase. It smelled like her grandma.

Before she took a sip from her cup, Norma dug into her pocket and slid several bills across the table. "For the honey."

Neva eyes crinkled as she smiled. "Thank you. But what I'd rather talk about is the fact that I think our visitor Chet has you discombobulated. I've never seen you so ruffled." She took a sip from her cup. "He's quite a handsome man. And, oh, that voice of his."

"How long is he staying?"

Neva cut a wedge from her scone. "He wasn't sure. He thought at least this week. He told me he had some exploring to do and wanted to look up an old friend." She finished chewing her bite and added, "He asked quite a bit about you. I daresay he might be smitten."

The heat rose in Norma's cheeks. She picked up her teacup to take a sip and hide her embarrassment. She set it back down and sighed. "I remind him of someone he once knew. It's just a case of mistaken identity."

Neva smiled and cut off another chunk from her scone. "If you say so, but I think there's more to it. There's a connection between the two of you. I can feel it."

CHAPTER 3

*M*onday Norma spent much of the day doing the household chores she had ignored for the last week as she'd poured all her energy into the all-class reunion. About midmorning she stopped to stir the soup in her slow cooker she was making for her lunch and start an audiobook to listen to while she went about her cleaning.

The Winey Widows were meeting tonight at Town Square Books and Norma had volunteered to bring dessert. Once she had the cottage sparkling and her laundry done, she made an apple cobbler with some apples she'd picked up at the farmers' market the week before.

As it baked, she took a shower to wash away all the dust and grime. She had worked up quite a sweat traipsing back and forth from her SUV to the shed in her backyard, where she labeled and placed all the totes with the reunion information in a neat stack. She ran her fingers through her hair to style it and chose a navy-blue cardigan, a color her mother had always told her made her dark gray eyes seem blue.

The buzzer on the oven sounded and she slipped into her loafers and plucked the bubbling cobbler from the oven. The aroma alone made her stomach growl. As she set it to cool, she glanced at the counter by the back door and saw the card the mayor had given with the bouquet last night. She had been in such a state, she'd put the flowers in water, gone to bed, and had forgotten about the card.

The envelope was so thick she had to take her letter opener to it. Once she slid it open, she found a lovely floral card. Inside were several gift certificates from local businesses and wonderful sentiments thanking her for making the all-class reunion such a success.

She took pride in being unemotional and practical, but tears stung the back of her throat as she read the card and studied each of the gift certificates. All her favorites were included—meals at the Crooked Porch, Bistro Claudine, Woody's Pizza, Cobblestone Deli & Bakery, coffee and drinks from Doc's, flowers from Bertie's, a full treatment at Curl Up & Dye, even gift cards from Town Square Books and Duncan's Hardware. The one from the Stitchin' Post for yarn and the generous gift card for spring plants at the nursery made her heart swell.

Now, she felt guilty for leaving before the concert was over. She should have made a point of thanking everyone. She'd try to make up for it and send each of the businesses and the mayor a thank-you card, but she'd have to tackle that tomorrow. She was going to be late.

She packed up the cobbler and her notebook and drove to Town Square Books. Despite worrying she was late, she was the first to arrive, just as Paige was closing the store. Paige hurried to the door and held it open while Norma balanced the cobbler, her purse, and notebook.

"Oh, that smells heavenly," said Paige, bending to get a whiff of the cobbler.

"Are you joining us tonight?" Paige had slid into the vacancy left by Margot at their weekly meetings, but since Reed had come back to Linden Falls, Paige didn't make as many meetings.

Paige smiled. "I am. Reed is on deadline, so he's busy writing every hour of the day." She wrinkled her nose. "I think he was secretly happy I had something to do tonight. He thinks he can finish his latest manuscript."

"Wonderful. We love having you."

Norma set the dish on the counter and selected a few packs of Paige's beautiful cards featuring her drawings of the Wishing Tree before Paige totaled out the register for the day. She slipped the cards into her purse and settled into a chair. Moments later, Agnes came through the door, toting a bag of wine bottles, followed by Jean and Cecilia, both carrying takeout bags from the Crooked Porch.

Norma wasn't a big hugger, but the other three

were all about hugging and she indulged them. As they set out the food selections, they raved about the weekend and the concert.

Agnes filled the wineglasses to the top, never spilling even a drop, and made sure everyone had their favorite. As always, she had on an attractive outfit, this one in a soft green. Her small stature always made Norma think of a pixie. Sometimes she envied Agnes and her petiteness and Jean and her tasteful clothes always paired with matching earrings, purses, and shoes. Cecilia, her oldest friend, both having started work the same year at the high school, was eclectic and did much of her clothes shopping at thrift stores. But she had a knack for putting random things together, even making her own jewelry, and pulled off looking younger in her stylish selections.

Norma ran her hand across her twill pants. Dowdy was the best word to describe her own wardrobe. From her comfortable shoes and shapeless cardigans to her unadorned earlobes, she was a fashion nightmare. She chuckled when she realized the biggest risk she had taken was pairing a blue cardigan with her tan pants.

She hadn't given her wardrobe or lack of fashion sense much thought until now. It must be the appearance of Chet Nelson. He had rattled her for sure. He'd also drudged up memories of the past. Too many memories. Too much pain.

She listened to her friends' chatter and laughter as they filled their plates. This was her happy place, her circle, her life. All the women in this room were her closest friends and even they didn't know her secret. Nobody alive knew. Nobody except Chet. And now he was here, in her world. His mere presence threatened upheaval in her quiet life.

Lost in her own worries, she hadn't been listening and Agnes's raised voice jolted her back to the conversation. "Sorry, Agnes, I was daydreaming. What did you say?"

The rest of the ladies giggled. "I was just saying that handsome drummer sure was asking about you last night. Maybe you were dreaming of him. Chet, right?"

Her heartrate increased as she did her best to downplay their interest in Chet. "I just reminded him of another girl he knew named Norma. I think he'd probably had a few too many."

Paige reached for her glass of wine. "He came by the store today with his beautiful golden, Willy. He and Gladys had a great time together. He seems like a nice guy. He said he's going to stay at Neva's place for the week and spend some time here. Said there was something at Linden Falls that just grabbed him and he couldn't bear to leave."

Jean nodded. "I ran into Neva earlier and she said he was asking quite a few questions about you. I think you might be what grabbed him."

Norma concentrated on her plate and waved away their excitement. "I think he's missing his youth and wishing I was someone else."

Agnes raised her brows. "You've never even dated

since Bob passed. I think it's high time you warm to the idea of male companionship."

Cecilia flung her head back and laughed. "Coming from a woman who has never suffered more than two days without so-called male companionship." She took a sip from her glass. "I, for one, admire Norma's independence and self-sufficiency. To each her own, I say. Whatever makes you happy."

Happy. That was a loaded word. Norma wasn't unhappy, but she wasn't sure she was truly happy. She was comfortable. Like her cardigan and loafers. She and Bob had been happy, but after she lost him, she hadn't felt the same. She'd enjoyed having a partner and had always felt safe with him. Without him, she was more cautious and more withdrawn. The Winey Widows had changed that, but she couldn't help feeling like she was missing something.

She had learned to adjust, and she wasn't one to whine and moan. She was tough and always faced adversity with strength and practicality. She also couldn't deny the little flutter of curiosity in her heart when she'd seen Chet at the reunion. She'd never imagined she would ever see him again. That part of her life was over, forgotten. Well, maybe not forgotten, just buried.

Her stomach in knots, Norma picked at the food on her plate while they discussed the plans for their spring trip. British Columbia was their destination of choice, in particular Vancouver Island and Victoria. Norma was dying to see Butchart Gardens and had come prepared with the research she had done on the area.

They were shooting for late April, when the tulips should be fabulous. Back in her comfort zone, Norma went through their lodging options, flights, and transportation costs. None of them wanted to drive, so Norma had found hotels and bed-and-breakfasts that offered shuttles to take them to tourist locations. They all agreed and liked the idea of flying to Seattle and taking the ferry to Vancouver Island.

Norma made notes of their final votes and promised to book their arrangements before the next meeting. She had such fun doing all the research, it was almost like getting to go on their trips twice. The others loved the fact that they didn't have to do anything except pay their share, since Norma enjoyed the planning task and always volunteered to do it.

Paige and Reed were considering a trip to the coast of Washington themselves. Despite all of them urging her to come with them, Paige decided it best to forgo the group trip but promised, if her plans changed, she'd join them.

With their business done, they finished off the open bottles of wine. Agnes had long ago established it sacrosanct to leave any bottles behind. Between the four original members, it was never a problem.

Jean, Cecilia, and Agnes left together, with Norma volunteering to help Paige clean up the leftovers. Paige boxed the food and put it in a bag, handing it to

Norma. "You barely ate a thing tonight. You take this home."

"Oh, that's sweet of you, but are you sure?"

"Trust me, Reed cooks enough that we have plenty of leftovers, even when Jed joins us for dinner. He enjoys cooking, which doesn't break my heart. It's a chore to me."

"I'll run this to my car and be right back to get the cobbler." She went through the door with Gladys staying behind, watching.

When she opened the door, she gasped when she saw Willy cuddled with Gladys and Chet standing at the counter talking to Paige. How long had she been gone and how had she not seen Chet?

He turned and smiled. "Hey, Norma. Paige said you'd be by for your meeting tonight. I was hoping to talk with you for a few minutes."

Norma looked past him at Paige, who shrugged, and gritted her teeth. "I'll leave you two to it. Just lock up like usual when you leave, Norma. Have a nice evening, Chet." She pointed to the counter. "I brewed a pot of tea for you." With Gladys following her, she disappeared behind the door that led into the house.

Norma stared at the door. She couldn't believe Paige would do that to her. *Traitor* was the first word that popped into her mind. She knew that wasn't fair, but her sweaty palms didn't bring much hope for the rest of the evening. Chet was proving to be quite stubborn and she wasn't going to be able to avoid him forever.

Despite no fire in the fireplace this time of year, she collected two mugs of tea and suggested they sit in the chairs near it. Willy's tail wagged as he sniffed at Norma but ultimately sat down at his master's feet.

Chet set his tea on the table between them. "I'm sorry to ambush you, Norma. I needed to see you and didn't want to show up at your house, so when I found out you'd be here tonight, I decided to stop by, hoping you'd feel safer to talk to me in a more public area."

"I'm not worried about my safety, Chet." Norma sighed. "It would seem you are quite determined."

He chuckled and petted Willy's ears. "I admit, you had me doubting myself after the concert, but then when I saw you at Neva's, I knew it was really you."

He pointed at his forehead. "That little scar you got playing in the championship game our senior year. I saw a hint of it that morning. I'm thrilled to see you again. Why are you so determined to hide from me?"

Norma touched her forehead with her finger. She had forgotten about the scar. It was so old, and she thought it hidden and faded. He must have been giving her quite the once-over to notice it.

She swallowed hard, her throat burning, and reached for a sip of tea before she answered. "I figured you would hate me. I ruined your life."

CHAPTER 4

*H*is deep blue eyes found hers. "At the time, I thought my life was ruined, but it turns out it just took a new path." He looked down at Willy. "I tried to find you. Your mom and dad said you'd decided to go to college elsewhere and they were sworn to secrecy."

She pressed her lips together. "I couldn't face Stockbridge, your family, my parents. There was no way I could have survived going home and all the looks and whispers that would follow me."

"It was an accident, Norma."

She shrugged. "I was the one driving."

"It couldn't have been avoided." His eyes softened. "Honestly, if anyone was to blame, it was Mitch."

Memories of that late summer day, just weeks before she was heading to college in Boston, flashed in her mind. She had been driving home from the store, running an errand for her mom. The sun was glaring in the windshield, making it hard to even see the street in front of her. All of a sudden, a figure flashed on the right and she'd slammed on the brakes, but it had been too late.

Chet cleared his throat. "We were all just goofing around, and Mitch shoved me a little too hard. I was trying to avoid that fire hydrant and ended up in the street. Honestly, it wouldn't have mattered who was driving. Even the police said it wasn't your fault."

"But I was driving. I was the reason the best baseball player Stockbridge had ever seen lost his college scholarship. I snuffed out your dreams and the dreams of everyone in town."

Her voice wobbled and she reached for her mug of tea. "I knew I couldn't stay there or go back. Just in the weeks that followed, I heard all the rumors and all the barbed comments."

"And you gave up your basketball scholarship?" He shook his head. "You didn't have to do that."

"Believe me, I had to. I couldn't go to the same college and think about what you had lost. The guilt was almost disabling."

"Where did you go?"

"I transferred to a small college in Vermont. Got a job waitressing and working in the library to put myself through school. Mom and Dad helped, of course, but I wouldn't let them pay for everything. It was my mistake. My choice. I needed to figure it out. Then, when I graduated, the librarian helped me get a job here at the high school. It all worked out. What about you? You're a musician?"

He grinned. "Nah, that's just for fun. Did you know your parents paid for me to go to college? It took a year for the surgeries and my leg to heal and then your dad came over and offered to pay for college. Boston was out of the question, but I ended up in a small college two hours east of Stockbridge. I got a degree in teaching—special education."

She shook her head, dumbfounded about her parents helping Chet with college. They had never said a word to her, but it did explain them cutting back on vacations and spending around that time. They were trying to atone for what she had done. She'd never given them a chance to tell her, since she wouldn't allow any conversation about Chet or the accident. She'd hung up the phone on more than one occasion when her mother tried to ease him into the conversation.

Still in shock, she willed herself to listen to Chet as he spoke about teaching. She'd had no clue her parents had helped him. She sighed. "Mom and Dad were always so kind and tried to convince me to put the accident behind me, but I never could." She gripped her mug of tea. "Special education is a true calling and difficult work."

"I loved it. I was also the high school baseball coach. I couldn't have asked for a better career. I mean that. I sometimes think that accident might have been the best thing that ever happened to me. It was meant to be."

Tears slid out of Norma's eyes. She pulled a tissue from the pocket of her cardigan and dabbed at her eyes. "I often wondered what happened to you, but I was too afraid to ask and had made up my mind that I was done with Stockbridge and my life there. I just wanted to forget it had ever happened. I was so ashamed."

He brought his hand to his chest. "That breaks my heart, Norma. You were such a sweet girl." He blushed. "I always had a little bit of a crush on you. That year I was home recovering, I used to dream you'd come back to check on me and we'd fall in love, get married, and live in Stockbridge."

She chuckled. "It must have been all the pain medication you were on."

"My mom and dad had nothing, so having your dad pay for my college was a true gift. Something I'll never forget. I've done my best to pay it forward and help other students."

"I had no idea he did that. My parents never told me." She shook her head. "That's on me. I made it clear I didn't want to know anything about you or hear about home." She reached for her tea again, not trusting her voice. "Truth is, I knew if they had talked about home, I might've caved and gone running back. I was so lonely and missed them, missed the town. I was afraid the slightest reminder would topple all my plans to make a new life where nobody knew me. I even changed my surname to my mother's maiden name. I wanted to disappear."

Chet looked devastated. "Wow, Norma. I am truly sorry I was the cause of such distress. Your mom and dad thought the sun rose and set on you. I know that. They never divulged your whereabouts or anything about you, but I could see it in their eyes and hear it in their voices—they missed you something fierce."

Tears fell onto her cheeks. "I know. I missed them as well. I was just so stubborn. So guilt-ridden. So young. When you're young, everything seems like the end of the world, you know?"

He nodded his head, reassuring her.

"They tried to talk me out of it, but in the end, they couldn't. They used to drive up and we'd meet in a little town halfway on the border of New Hampshire and Vermont for visits. That worked well until they got older, and I couldn't persuade them to move from Stockbridge, closer to me."

"I'm so sorry, Norma. It sounds like that accident did far more damage to you than it did to me."

His words landed like a glass of icy water in her face. She'd never considered his life had been fulfilling and happy. In her mind, he was the young man who'd had his hopes dashed, his leg injured so severely he had a permanent limp, and his career over before it even began. A town tragedy caused by hers truly.

After college and moving to Linden Falls, she had put him out of her mind. She couldn't endure thinking about him, which only brought her guilt and depression back to the surface.

"You know, all young athletes dream of going pro. Getting picked up by a major team and having a famous life. Especially small-town boys with humble beginnings." He reached again for Willy. "The chances of all that actually happening are somewhere between slim and none. I wish I would have found you years ago and put your mind at ease."

She shook her head. "I can't believe you've forgiven me. I just imagined you hating me, resenting me, forever."

"Nothing could be further from the truth. I'm just sorry you gave up your own dreams and your basketball scholarship."

She dabbed at her eyes. "I never had pro dreams; it was just a great way to have college paid for and continue playing the game I loved."

"I think you've punished yourself enough. You gave up so much more than I did. Your family. Your home. Your identity, even."

"It was the best solution at the time. The articles in the papers, and not just Stockbridge's, they were all over, pushed me to the brink. I didn't want to be the young woman who was responsible for ending your baseball career. I just wanted to disappear."

He glanced out the window to the quiet street. "Mission accomplished."

She took a deep breath, letting some of the stress and angst she had been holding for over fifty years escape with it. "So, tell me more about your life of teaching and coaching. Did you marry? Have children?"

He nodded. "I did marry a wonderful woman. Nancy. We had two children, both girls. Nancy passed away just after Christmas. Cancer." He paused before adding, "I'm also a grandpa to five."

"Where did you teach, back in Stockbridge?"

He shook his head. "Nah, I ended up getting a job in Concord, New Hampshire. Spent my whole career there and loved it. Getting to be the baseball coach was the icing on the cake. It let me be involved with the sport I loved, albeit in a different role. Like I said, it all worked out for the best." He explained about his music hobby and how he started using it in his classroom, bringing in his guitar to play for the kids. He noticed it calmed them and they enjoyed it, so he kept at it.

"I played the drums for the Rockin' Chairs but love the guitar and piano most."

"Ah, that explains why you named your dog Willy Nelson." Norma laughed.

"Different spelling, of course, but yes. I love his old songs." He continued telling her more about his life and career.

Her eyes, looking more blue than usual, sparkled as she listened to his story. "You don't know how happy that makes me. How relieved."

"So, tell me more about your life. I noticed the students at the reunion saying you were Mrs. Braxton, so I assume you married?"

"Yes, I married Bob not long after moving to Linden Falls. I rented a room in a house here and he came to fix the washing machine. His dad had an appliance repair business. That's how we met. Not especially romantic, but he was a wonderful man. He passed away several years ago."

"No children?" Chet asked.

She shook her head. Another regret, though not one she could control. They had wanted to have children, but after years of trying and failing, the local doctor suggested a specialist, who discovered Norma had a problem and would never conceive. It had been a blow at the time, but she and Bob learned to adjust and had a fulfilling life together. "I do envy you having grandchildren. I think that would be something I would enjoy."

He reached for her hand and she gripped it in hers. "To think I almost didn't come with Joe. He's been trying to get me to get out more. Since Nancy. I wasn't all that keen on coming to some tiny town in Vermont, but like so much of my life, it was meant to be."

She smiled. "I should have been braver years ago."

"I think you're plenty brave, Norma. It takes courage to leave everything you know and love to strike out on your own. I'm not surprised, though. You always were strong and independent."

Her brows arched. "Really?"

"Yes, really. I think it's high time you forgive yourself. Stop hiding from the past. Life is short, as we both know." He squeezed her hand tighter.

When he smiled at her, something fluttered inside.

Something she hadn't felt for a very long time. It was like fifty years had been erased and she saw the handsome young man she remembered, right in front of her, holding her hand.

"I'm here for the week and would like nothing more than to spend that time with you. Maybe you could show me around and take me to the famous Linden Falls I've heard so much about. What do you say?"

She swallowed the lump that had formed in her throat. "I'd like that very much, Chet."

"How about I pick you up tomorrow and we'll have lunch, then you can take me on a tour?"

"That would be perfect. Let me jot my address down for you."

He laughed and held up his hand as he rose from his chair. "No need. Neva told me where you lived, and I drove by today."

She accepted his offer of a hand up and walked him and Willy to the door. He rested his hand on the doorknob and then turned back toward her. "Thank you for talking to me, Norma. I feel so much better having had the chance to explain things."

She brought her hand to her chest. "I'm the one who should be thanking you. I was worrying about avoiding you all week. I'm glad you were persistent, and I'll have to ask Paige for forgiveness. I glared at her for telling you I'd be here tonight. But you've lifted a heavy weight from my shoulders."

"Until tomorrow, then." He ushered Willy out the door. "Have a good evening, Norma."

She watched him walk across the square and noticed Neva standing under the Wishing Tree, the lights strung across the square illuminating her figure and her long silvery hair. Not many women her age could pull off that look, but on her it was beautiful and matched her almost ethereal presence. Norma admired the woman. They couldn't be more opposite, with Neva's free-spirited personality and penchant for her strong intuition and Norma's down-to-earth practicality. Despite all their differences, Norma considered her one of her best friends.

Neva waved at her, and even in the low light, Norma saw her friend's knowing smile.

CHAPTER 5

*E*arly Tuesday morning, Norma found herself sitting in Vera's chair at the Curl Up & Dye. When she got home the night before, she'd taken a chance and put it in a call, knowing Vera sometimes worked late. Having tried to talk her into something besides her normal trim for years, Vera was thrilled that Norma was interested in a bit of a hair makeover and volunteered to come in early for her.

Chet's visit and their conversation last night had prompted something inside Norma. His words about her hiding from the past and enjoying her life had resonated. Although she'd had a happy life, enjoyed her job, and loved Bob, she hadn't lived it to the fullest. The cloud of her past had always hovered over her. There were times, like when she was with her friends from the Winey Widows, the sun broke through, but most of her life, she had spent simply existing and getting through the days, the weeks, the months, and the years.

Her past, the dreaded accident, all that it brought with it, had hung like a brick around her neck. Today, for the first time since she was eighteen, she felt lighter and happier, maybe even hopeful. While the snip-snip of Vera's scissors moved across her hair, Norma pondered that very idea.

Hope.

That was what she had been without for so long.

Sure, she looked forward to the trips and outings with the Winey Widows and they'd all taken Paige under their wings to help her after Margot's passing, but her life had been devoid of that one special spark. Her future held only the careful routine and order she had established, not hopefulness.

Today was different. Chet had given her a gift. She didn't have to worry or hide any longer. He had forgiven her long ago and she was finally free of the horrible guilt she had carried each day since that fateful day.

She stole a glance in the mirror. It was hard to know how old Vera was. Norma knew she was younger than she was, but it was hard to pinpoint her generation. Nobody could remember her natural hair color or even if they knew it. She changed her hair color and style on a whim. She always matched her glittery eye shadow, framed by thick and long dark lashes, with her outfits, whether they be purple or green. On anyone else, the heavy makeup and dyed hair would be garish, but Vera always looked gorgeous.

It wasn't a style Norma would like, nor could she

fathom wasting the amount of time Vera must have spent each morning, just getting ready, but it fit the beautician. Vera was ageless and perfectly happy to let her clients keep their plain old mousy hair if they wanted, but her big eyes lit up with excitement when she was allowed to create something new. She said she thought of herself as an artist and hair as a sculpture.

Norma looked out the window while Vera blew her hair dry, dispensed some product that smelled liked sandalwood with a hint of coconut across her hands and styled Norma's hair with her fingers, and then used a curling iron. She made sure Norma was facing away from the mirror as she finished. Vera stepped back to admire it and then said, "How would you feel about just a hint of color on your cheeks and some lip gloss?"

Norma hadn't worn makeup since high school, and even then, it hadn't been much. She started to resist and then thought again. "Oh, why not? Just don't overdo it."

Norma hated the look of heavy makeup, especially on older women who had those dirty-looking orange rings of it along their chin and neck. She preferred a more subtle and clean look.

She followed Vera's instructions to close her eyes, then sat still as Vera's soft fingers and specialty brushes glided over her skin. Vera finished her off with a bit of mascara and then twirled the chair around so Norma could get a look in the mirror.

Norma was flabbergasted.

The reflection staring back at her couldn't be hers. She slid from the chair and stepped forward, closer to the mirror to get a better look. Her hair was gorgeous. It looked thicker and shinier than she could ever remember. Vera had rambled on about lowlights and highlights and Norma told her to do whatever she thought best. She had no clue what any of it meant, but the result was more than she'd expected.

She couldn't pry her eyes away from the mirror. Women always talked about a new hairdo or makeup taking years off them and Norma had discounted such foolishness, but she couldn't deny what was staring her in the face.

Vera's eyebrows arched as she cast a quizzical look Norma's way.

"Well? What do you think?"

Norma's eyes found her, standing in the mirror behind her. Norma touched her fingertips to her hair. "I can't believe it, Vera. I love it. I only hope I can style it like you have."

"It's a piece of cake. When we have more time, pop in and I'll show you the tricks. If you've got a blow dryer and curling iron, you're set." She reached for a travel-sized bottle of the lovely smelling oil she had used on Norma's hair and handed it to her. "This stuff is magic. Just use a tiny drop or two and run it through your hair after you blow-dry it."

Norma took the bottle and turned from side to side, checking her face. "Honestly, it doesn't look like I'm wearing makeup, except for the color in my cheeks and lips. You've outdone yourself, Vera."

She beamed and hugged Norma. "I'm just so thrilled and honored you allowed me to give you a new look. It's just fabulous."

Norma dug in her bag and retrieved the thank-you card and homemade pumpkin bread she had placed in it early in the morning. She handed Vera the bread, with its mouthwatering cinnamon and clove scent, wrapped with a glittery orange ribbon, and placed the thank-you card on top of it. "I can't thank you enough for the gift certificate and for squeezing me in."

"Just seeing you smile and your beautiful eyes light up is all I need." Vera hugged her again and sent her on her way. "Plus, I've been itching to do this to you for years."

Norma laughed.

She felt lighter somehow as she walked down the sidewalk to her car. She did a double take when she spied her reflection in the shop windows along Main Street. The new layered style, with the modern wispy bangs and subtle streaks of color that looked so natural, gave her the boost she needed.

When she got back to her cottage, there was a parcel at the front door. Her name was written on one of the papers Neva used for the Wishing Tree and she recognized Neva's script.

She toted it inside and opened it up to discover a beautiful denim jacket in a deep plum color with a flowy scarf. Neva had included a short note letting her know she was going through some items and clearing out and thought this color would be perfect on her. She suggested she wear it with a turtleneck and jeans.

Norma smiled as she set about brewing a cup of tea. Having left so early, she had missed her morning ritual. She held up the beautiful scarf, noting the gorgeous shades of purples and blues, along with a metallic gold thread that ran through it. Neva wore scarves all the time and always looked so elegant.

Well, Norma had plenty of turtlenecks and jeans. They were her uniform in the fall and winter months. She had two cups of tea while she vacillated between a navy or a charcoal turtleneck. She had never spent so much time choosing an outfit. It was ridiculous. Seeing Chet again had turned her into a goofy teenaged girl.

Not having been on an outing, or daresay even a date, with a man since Bob had courted her, a sense of nervousness crept over her. It wasn't an actual date, was it? Nah, she was much too old for dating. Just two old friends reconnecting.

She decided on the navy, since it did seem to bring out the blue flecks in her eyes. She was dressed and ready in plenty of time to finish her thank-you notes. As soon as she sealed the last one and added it to the pile, there was a soft tap on her front door.

She grabbed her bag along with a jacket and opened the door to the smiling face of Chet. When he saw her, his jaw dropped and then a slow grin filled his face, showcasing his dimples. "Aren't you a sight for sore eyes?"

"Ah, I had a hair appointment this morning." She locked the door behind her and took the arm he offered.

"Well, my compliments to her. I think you're more beautiful today than when we were in school."

Norma giggled. Yes, she actually giggled, like a young schoolgirl. She brought her hand to her lips. What had come over her?

He pointed to the huge SUV he was driving. "My rental chariot awaits." He held open her door and she saw Willy stick his head in between the two front seats. "Willy is joining us on our explorations, but only if it's okay with you. He needs some exercise, but Paige said she'd let him stay at the bookstore with Gladys if need be."

"Any friend of Gladys is a friend of mine." She reached to pet him and swore he winked at her.

After Chet waited for her to settle and shut her door, he hurried around the front of the vehicle and slid behind the wheel. "I picked up a picnic basket from Cobblestone Deli and thought since it's such a beautiful day we might be able to enjoy a lunch up at the falls. Does that sound okay?"

"What a wonderful idea." It brought back memories of when she and Bob had first been dating and after they married. She had often put together a quick basket and they'd take the short hike to the falls and enjoy a summer dinner there. She hadn't been up there in years.

The falls were walkable from a short trail in town

and took only minutes with Chet driving them. After opening Norma's door for her, Chet lugged the picnic basket and kept an eye on Willy, who liked to hold his leash in his mouth as he trotted along the paved trail that led to the actual falls.

Linden Falls was subtle, not to be confused with some of Vermont's famous ones of the thundering, jaw-dropping variety that cascaded hundreds of feet. While not dramatic, they were still awe-inspiring and beautiful to see, as the water gently fell over the tables of gray rock, gathering in several small wells along the way, before ending in a large and inviting pool filled with pristine water. The resulting swimming hole formed by the falls was quite popular with the local kids from Linden Falls, and since school hadn't quite started, there were a few of them enjoying it today.

The setting was quiet and peaceful, surrounded by the huge green trees. Some of the early bloomers were beginning to change their leaves and a few specks of the gorgeous autumn colors splashed among them.

Chet pointed at a picnic table that gave them a view of the falls and led the way.

He placed the basket atop the table and reached for Willy's leash. "I'm going to take this guy for a bit of a walkabout so he can get rid of some of his inquisitive energy. Do you want to set up lunch while we're gone or join us?"

"I'll get lunch ready. I'm dying to see what's in that basket." She smiled and watched as Chet led Willy to the trail that would take them down to one of the middle pools, where there would be less chance for Willy to be enticed by the kids who were swimming. She didn't know much about golden retrievers but knew Margot always had a hard time keeping Gladys out of the water.

She unearthed the treasures in the basket, including cloth napkins, actual plates, and stainless-steel utensils. Her mouth watered as she eyed the mini charcuterie board filled with bite-sized nibbles of cheese and fruit and carefully unwrapped the tight cellophane that held it all in place. The aroma of Cobblestone's freshly baked bread covering roasted turkey and cranberries was heavenly. Along with containers of salads, she found the bakery's famous goat cheese and maple bacon slices. Bottles of water and wine plus a box of bite-sized brownies and cookies topped it all off.

At this rate, they wouldn't need dinner. By the time Willy and Chet turned the last corner on the trail, both smiling as they made their way back to Norma, she had everything arranged on the table. She put the place settings next to each other so they could both have a view of the falls.

Willy greeted Norma with a hefty wag of his tail and then settled down next to Chet. "Wow, this all looks great, doesn't it?" he said, taking a few cubes of cheese from the platter.

"You did a wonderful job with the selections. I wasn't sure I was going to be able to wait for you two to get back before digging into it."

He reached for the bottle of water and poured himself a glass. "Water or wine for you?"

"Water is perfect."

"Just for the record, I had absolutely nothing to do with picking out the contents. I just told them I wanted the best as I was trying to impress an old friend of mine." He winked and took a bite of his sandwich. "Aah, that is delicious."

While they ate, they chatted about their lives. Norma was curious. "So, how do you keep busy now that you're retired from teaching? Do you play in the band often?"

Chet reached for another helping of the loaded potato salad. "Losing Nancy has been a huge blow, so I'm trying to find myself again. We have a beautiful home on a couple of acres outside of town. Nancy's family is from there and she never wanted to live anywhere else, but without her, I'm not sure I want to stay there. Too many memories, you know?"

She nodded her head and finished the bite of delectable blend of sweet and savory goat cheese and bacon slice. "That's understandable. All the reminders and memories, especially in those early days, were difficult." Her mind wandered a bit and then she added, "Bob had always talked about moving to Florida one day, but he passed away before we could make that happen. Now, without him, I'm not sure that's something I would tackle."

"Wow, Florida was on our radar as well. While Nancy would never give up her home, I had been making some headway into convincing her we could spend winters and enjoy the sun down there."

"Do your children live near you?" she asked, popping a brownie bite into her mouth.

"Our two daughters moved out of the area after they got married. One's outside of Providence and the other near Boston. They come home for holidays and visits, but not often. They have jobs and families and it's harder and harder to coordinate. I'm not much of a big-city guy, so while I could go and visit them, I honestly don't want to deal with the traffic and people."

She bobbed her head. "I agree with you on that. I've never loved big cities. Sometimes, I'm glad I skipped Boston for college. As much of a blow as it was at the time, it's turned out to be a good thing. The small town and smaller college were perfect for me and made me feel at home when I needed it most. They led me here. It's home."

"It's a beautiful town, so picturesque and hasn't been subjected to growth like so many of the small towns around here. You made a good choice." He popped two more cubes of cheese into his mouth. "I guess I didn't really answer your question about what I do to keep busy. Willy and I have been doing quite a bit of walking, making a big loop around the property each morning and evening. I do a little volunteer work at the school, usually go to coffee each morning with some old buddies, and tinker in my workshop."

He reached for a brownie. "I'm fortunate in that I retired many years ago, and while I get a pension, I live off the royalties of my invention. Years ago, when I was coaching, I designed a pitching machine and, with the help of a couple of friends, ended up getting a patent and selling it."

"Wow," said Norma, her eyes wide. "That's remarkable and so exciting."

He grinned. "Like I tried to tell you before, my life has been wonderful and fulfilling, and while the accident was horrible at the time, it put me on a different path. The one I was meant to follow. The one that led me to you."

His words made her heart do a little flip, deep in her chest, and her eyes widened as he continued. "I never thought about playing an instrument, but a couple of the teachers at the school really wanted to start a band and I got into it. Took some lessons. The instructor told me I had a natural ability, could play by ear, apparently. It just sort of fell in my lap. I even tried to get out of coming here to play. I was just a replacement, but Joe kept bugging me. I guess it's a good thing he did and that he prodded me into coming over to the registration table."

He took a long swallow of water and then winked at Norma. "I think fate has conspired all these years to get me here, for this moment, with you."

CHAPTER 6

*T*hey spent the rest of the afternoon talking, sharing all that had transpired in their lives over the last fifty years. Chet flipped through his phone and shared pictures of his family and his beautiful wife. He lingered over one photo of Nancy in particular, her kind eyes and big smile filling the screen.

"For me, it was love at first sight. Nancy came from a prominent family, and as you know, I came from very humble beginnings, so I was pretty nervous about meeting her mom and dad. As it turned out, they were as nice as she was, and when I asked for her hand, they were thrilled. She and her mom planned a huge wedding. Not my cup of tea, but I didn't care as long as Nancy was happy. We had a wonderful life. Not without a few snags, but all I have are wonderful memories."

Norma stared at the photo. "She was lovely, as are your daughters and grandchildren. I'd say you have much more than just memories." Norma didn't have a family and Bob had passed before taking photos on her phone was popular.

"I don't have such a fairy tale to share. Bob and I fell in love quietly. No fanfare, just a simple proposal, under the Wishing Tree. We got married at the court-house and celebrated with an expensive dinner at a restaurant that is no longer in business. No honey-moon or fancy trip, just moved into the cottage and started our life together."

Her mind wandered to those early days. "He was a good man. A kind man. A generous man. So, while ours wasn't a love-at-first-sight sort of story, it was a deep and enduring love. Sometimes I miss that. Especially when I see how sweet Henry is to Neva. He's courting her in such a lovely and old-fashioned way. It's so romantic. It's nice to see them both so happy but, at the same time, bittersweet when it reminds me of all I've lost."

He reached for her hand. "It's easy to let the loss overtake us. Some days, I'm not sure I'll survive it. I just try to remember that Nancy would want me to keep living and to be happy and I'm sure Bob would want the same for you." He brought her hand to his lips and brushed them over the tops of her knuckles. "I'm just thankful I found you again. It's been wonderful to see you and spend time with you."

His touch sent a tingle through her arm and all the way to her toes.

After spending most of the afternoon at Linden

Falls, chatting, and exploring the many trails around the falls, Norma grew tired. She and Chet packed up the remnants of their picnic and Willy and headed back to town.

He pulled up to Norma's cottage and turned off the ignition before turning toward her. "This was the best day I've had in a very long time. Thank you for spending it with me. I don't want to sound too forward, but we have fifty years to catch up on and I'd love it if you'd consider joining me tonight for dinner."

For once, Norma let her heart speak instead of her brain. "That sounds lovely, but how about we just have dinner here at my house? We have plenty of leftovers and I have cobbler."

He grinned and reached for her hand. "You had me even before you mentioned cobbler." Once again, like a true gentleman, he stepped out and came around to open her door, then walked her to the front porch. "I'm going to grab a little catnap and I'll come back around seven o'clock if that works for you."

She opened the door and he followed her inside, toting the picnic basket. "That sounds great. You can just put that on the counter." She led the way through to her small kitchen and added, "Be sure and bring Willy Nelson. He's welcome to join us."

Chet turned and grinned at her as he made his way out of the kitchen. "He'd love that. See you soon, Norma."

Norma smiled as she began unloading the basket. Once she had all the leftovers put away, she added soap to her sponge and washed and dried the dinnerware before returning it back in the basket. While she worked, she reflected on what a wonderful day she had enjoyed. She'd been missing out on the beauty of the falls, but after today's visit, she might have to incorporate them into her walking routine.

Finding Chet, or actually Chet finding her, after all these years was almost a miracle. Maybe, like he said, it was meant to be. She wiped down the counters and gazed around her spotless kitchen. She didn't have anything more to do and still had well over two hours before Chet would return.

Chet's mention of a nap made her long for one. She hated risking her new hairdo, but the thought of a few minutes of rest lured her to her bedroom. Once again thinking of her grandma, she dug through her cabinet in the bathroom and found what she knew was there. She pinned the pink satin scarf around her hair before lying down, pulling the velvety throw she favored over her legs, and gently placing her head on her pillow.

She willed herself to stay in one position and closed her eyes as both the excitement and the exhaustion it had created settled over her.

WHEN NORMA WOKE, her heart thudded in her chest. She glanced at the clock on her night table and saw she had only slept for an hour, but it seemed like she had been asleep all night. She sprang from the bed, straightened the comforter and pillow, and took down the scarf to inspect her hair.

It was no worse for wear. Her grandma had been onto something.

When it came to makeup, she had next to nothing. She made a mental note to stop by Vera's when she wasn't busy and get a list of the basics. Never having given much credence to the articles in magazines or women on television talking about the boost it gave them to wear makeup, and having a bias against wasting time and money, Norma was shocked at how much her mini makeover had boosted her confidence.

Maybe there was more to all that than she'd thought. Or maybe it was reconnecting with Chet. Whatever it was, she felt invigorated for the first time in years. By this time of day, she was tired and looking forward to snuggling in and reading or watching something on television, but tonight she was having company.

Her social outings were usually limited to going places with the Winey Widows or stopping by and having tea at Neva's. Part of her hated to be so excited to spend an evening with Chet. She worried about how empty her life would be when he left Linden Falls.

Stop it, Norma.

She shut her eyes and took a deep breath. She'd read enough self-help books to recognize she didn't practice living in the moment, always worrying about tomorrow.

She went about gathering the leftovers to make a

buffet of sorts on her small kitchen dining table. She eyed the wooden hutch that held her nicest dishes. She kept them there to save them for special occasions. They were like new. Norma took out two place settings and two wineglasses and rinsed them off with hot water.

Tonight, she would immerse herself in the here and now and enjoy every minute with Chet, dining off the dishes she had saved all these years that were destined to end up at some thrift shop when she was dead.

She added the flowers the mayor had given her to the center of the table and stood back to admire it. She'd never be able to pull off what Jean and Agnes could do with fashion or décor, but the table looked lovely and inviting. Going forward, she might just have to eat off her good dishes every night.

She retrieved an old blanket from the linen cupboard and wrapped a large floor pillow she never used inside of it, to make a comfortable nest for Willy on the floor near the dining table. Since she didn't have a dog bed, it was the best she could do for him.

She fussed with the table a bit more until everything was in order and even lit a couple of candles she had never used. The table gleamed and the candlelight added a hint of ambience.

She checked the clock and frowned. He was fifteen minutes late. She was a stickler for being on time, always early, but had learned not everyone shared her penchant for promptness. She brewed a cup of tea and settled into her recliner in the living room. She picked up the book she had been reading, hoping to calm her nerves.

When she realized she'd read the same page five times, she checked her watch. Thirty minutes. That was at the edge of fashionably late.

After an hour, Norma opened the front door and walked out to the edge of the sidewalk, looking up and down the street. It was quiet and there was no sign of Chet's rental.

She returned to the kitchen and sighed. The wax had melted and puddled in the glass candleholders. She reached across and blew them out, leaving a thin trail of smoke snaking up to the ceiling. Her heart hurt. She tried not to let the sense of betrayal she felt overwhelm her.

Something must have come up. Something that kept him from the courtesy of a phone call. Did he even have her phone number? She didn't have his. Maybe something happened with one of his daughters or Willy. Maybe she should call Neva and see what she knew. That would just lead to having to explain things she wasn't ready to discuss.

She was already tired of the what-if game.

Her appetite was gone. She stowed all the leftovers in the fridge, returned her good dishes to the hutch, and covered up the apple cobbler.

Even her beloved books couldn't tempt her tonight. She made sure the doors were locked, turned out the lights, and padded down the short hallway to her bedroom.

She changed into her pajamas, and as she washed her face, she recognized the sadness in her eyes. She felt like a schoolgirl waiting for the cutest boy in class to call her. It was ridiculous to get so wrapped up in the moment. Especially at her age.

She brushed her teeth and applied lotion to her face. The satin scarf was still on the vanity. She sighed and pinned it around her hair. She loved her hair and wasn't going to let her disappointment ruin it.

As she slid under the blanket, defeat settled over her. She tried to do what she had done for years and lock away any disappointment and look at the bright side of things. She had enjoyed a lovely day, a perfect one, and even more important, learned she hadn't ruined Chet's life. Today had been a fluke and she had a good life, albeit quiet and at times lonely.

She reached over and flicked the button on her CD player. The familiar voice of Jo Stafford filled the room. She and Bob had loved all her songs, but especially "You Belong to Me," and when that song began, tears leaked from her eyes. She closed them, transported back in time, letting the melody wash over her and comfort her.

One perfect day might be all she would get. She'd take it.

CHAPTER 7

*T*he next morning, Norma set out on her walk, like usual. She meandered around the neighborhood and then ventured to town square. As she walked by Neva's, she noticed Chet's rental car was parked out front. She glared at it. That meant he was still in town.

She continued her routine and made a loop down Main Street, trying not to dwell on being stood up last night. She loved the quiet of the morning, when all the shops were closed and the streets were still. The smell of coffee drifted out of Doc's and Cobblestone had a small line at the bakery counter, but the rest of the town was still sleeping.

She noticed the shop that had been empty for a couple of months now had brown paper covering the windows and saw a woman coming out of the door. "Good morning," said Norma.

"Hello there," said the woman, her blond hair glistening in the morning sun.

"I'm so glad to see something new moving in. I'm Norma, by the way. When are you opening?"

The woman's eyebrows rose and she extended her hand. "Lovely to meet you, Norma. I'm Millie King. I have to be open soon. I'm taking over the village post office contract from Fisher Drugs. I'm opening an office supply store and will be transferring the post office counter here. I'm going to try to carry a few art supplies as well. I'm keeping it simple and calling it the Post Office."

Norma smiled. "I like simple. Welcome to Linden Falls, Millie. Fisher Drugs is so busy, I can see why he's wanting to get rid of the postage area. They have so many things in there, I'm sure it takes up too much time."

Millie nodded. "Exactly. They're plenty busy, and as a new business, I could use the extra revenue from the postal service, plus I'm sure my store will be less crowded than a drugstore." She pointed above her. "This place has the bonus of the living space above it, so it's a good fit for me and my dog."

Norma noticed only the tip of a snout at the edge of the brown paper covering the glass in the front door. "Oh, yes. In the past, so many shopkeepers lived above their businesses and it seems very efficient. I do hope you enjoy it. It will be wonderful to have office supplies in town. I'll be back when you're open. Nice to meet you."

Millie waved goodbye as Norma continued on her walk.

As she made her way back by Neva's, she did a double take. Through the glass of the front door, she saw Willy and his tail wagged when she met his eyes. Moments later, the door opened and Neva waved her hand at her. "Norma, could you do me a favor?"

"Sure, what can I do?"

"Would you take Willy down to Jed at the hardware store?"

"Sure, I can do that. What's going on? Where's Chet?"

"Oh, dear, I thought he probably called you. He said he had a wonderful day up at the falls. He wasn't feeling well and Henry was here visiting before dinner and we urged him to let him drive him to the hospital."

Norma's heart sank and her legs felt wobbly. Neva reached for her friend's hand. "Don't worry. He's fine and they're on their way home, but I can't get breakfast ready with Willy glued to me. He's been pacing and whining, worrying about his master, I'm sure."

"You're sure Chet's okay?"

Neva nodded. "From what Henry said, it sounds like the doctors did a bunch of tests but decided his symptoms were due to medication. They're both tired from spending all night there, but he's going to be fine. Don't worry."

Norma took Willy's leash in her hand. "I feel horrible but am relieved. Chet was due to come over

for dinner last night and when he didn't show up..."
Norma's voice tightened, and she couldn't continue.

"Oh, Norma. I'm sorry you were thinking the worst.
I'm sure he would have called if he could have."

Norma nodded. "He doesn't have my number. I
realized that last night. I don't have his either."

Neva smiled and her eyes sparkled in the morning
sunlight. "There you go. That explains it all. I'll be sure
and tell him you stopped by and I'll give him your
number."

Norma sighed and smiled at her friend. "Thank
you. I'm just glad he's okay. Tell him to get some rest
and give me a call later. I'll drop Willy off right now."

"Wonderful. Jed said he could hang with Bentley
this morning and I'm sure Gladys will join the party.
Chet's going to need to get some sleep when he gets
back, so that will give him a break."

Norma set off down the block, with Willy by her
side. She murmured her reassurances to the dog,
letting him know Chet was okay and would be back
soon. Never having had a dog, she wasn't sure if he
understood, but the dog's ears perked up when she said
Chet's name and it made her feel better to say it.

Jed was at the counter and Bentley dashed from
behind it as soon as she and Willy stepped closer. "Hey,
Norma. Looks like these two are excited for a playdate.
I'll keep my eye on them and they can play in the back
office. I told Neva I'd bring him back by closing time if
Chet hasn't come to pick him up by then."

"It's nice of you to keep him. I know he appreciates it."

He smiled at her and then laughed at the two dogs mauling each other. "It's no problem. They'll have fun and keep each other busy."

He gave Bentley the command to follow him and both dogs hurried to his side and he led them toward the back of the store.

Satisfied her mission was complete, Norma set off for home.

She spent the rest of the morning organizing the Winey Widows' trip to Vancouver Island and figuring out the best flights and booking their lodging, including a shuttle that would take them to the ferry terminal. The bed-and-breakfast in Victoria would send their complementary van when the women arrived.

The innkeeper offered to set up a tour that would transport the group to Butchart Gardens, since she was able to offer a discount on the package through a local tour company. They were planning to take in many of the tourist areas near Victoria Harbour and the innkeeper assured Norma it was easy to get trans-portation around the city if their shuttle couldn't accommodate them.

Her stomach grumbled and she checked the clock. It was lunchtime and she hadn't eaten since yesterday. She needed more than the two pots of tea she had sipped while working on the vacation itinerary.

She opened the fridge and eyed her options. She

ignored all the picnic leftovers she had put away and scanned the shelves. Breakfast sounded good. She scrambled a couple of eggs, popped in some toast, and brewed more tea.

After tidying the kitchen, she emailed the Winey Widows with the information about the trip and their share of the costs. With that huge task accomplished, Norma poured herself a fresh cup of tea and slid into her recliner. She planned to read a few chapters in her book but didn't even get through one before her eyes closed.

⫸⫸

THE KNOCK on her front door jarred her awake. A glance at the clock made her gasp. She had slept for over two hours. She hurried to the door and found Chet holding a huge burgundy chrysanthemum in a copper planter with Willy at his side, the dog's tail wagging in quick arcs.

"Norma," he said, extending the plant. "I'm so sorry for missing our dinner last night. Neva said she saw you this morning and told you about my medical drama. I came to beg your forgiveness and see if I could treat you to dinner tonight."

She smiled and took the plant from him. "That is gorgeous. Thank you. I think it's perfect for my porch." She set it next to a painted bench she often sat on during the evenings. She motioned Chet inside the house, noticing how his crisp blue shirt brought out his eyes. When he passed by her, the scent of sandalwood and lemon tickled her nose. He smelled incredible.

She led him and Willy to the living room. "May I offer you something to drink?"

He held up his hand. "I'm fine for now. I was going to call and thought I'd rather face you in person and ask your forgiveness. My absence was unavoidable, and once at the hospital, it was chaotic."

"All is forgiven. I trust you're feeling better?" She moved the blanket she had been using to the arm of her chair and could only hope her hair didn't look like she'd been sleeping for the last two hours.

He nodded. "I was incredibly dizzy yesterday afternoon, my heart was beating really fast, and I just felt odd. I probably should have just rested, but Henry and Neva thought it best to get checked out. Poor Henry ended up staying there with me all night long." He sighed. "Anyway, it ended up being related to my blood pressure medication. The doctor recommended a change and also said I was dehydrated, so they hooked me up to a drip, ran all their tests, waited for all the consultations, and finally let me go early this morning."

"Well, that's good news, at least."

"I've been sleeping since we got back here and hope poor old Henry recovers. I felt horrible having him drive me, but he insisted."

"Oh, he's a very kind person. I'm sure he didn't mind. It's what we do around here."

"I feel awful about last night. I planned to call you and then realized I didn't have your number. Henry wasn't in the room with me, so I couldn't ask him, and then I remembered you hadn't told anyone here about our past connection and I didn't want to do anything to upset you. Anyway, it was a mess."

"Please don't worry. I'm just glad you're okay." Norma rose from her chair and made her way to the kitchen, returning with a fresh cup of tea and a large glass of water for Chet. "Drink up. It sounds like you need to drink more water."

He smiled. "Yes, ma'am."

"About dinner, I've got everything saved, so why don't we just nibble on that tonight and stay in for the evening. You can rest up from your adventure and I'll make sure you drink all the water I can force down you."

He leaned back in the chair. "That sounds like a wise idea. The doctor wanted me to take it easy for a couple of days."

She made another trip to the kitchen and returned toting the pillow she had fashioned into a bed for Willy. "I put this together last night for Willy." She set it down on the floor between the two recliners. "We'll see if he likes it."

"Aww, look at that, sweet boy. Norma made you a nice bed." The dog sniffed at the pillow and circled it a few times before plopping down on it. Chet glanced up at Norma. "I think he's quite happy with it and that was kind of you to think of him."

Norma glanced at the big dog perched on her old pillow. "He's a sweet one and reminds me so much of

Gladys. I never had a dog, but spending time with my late friend, Margot, I learned what loyal friends they can be."

He bent down to ruffle Willy's ears. "You ought to get one. They're loads of fun. In fact, Willy was bred just last month, and I get first dibs on a puppy from the litter. They'll be ready around Christmas."

Norma's eyes widened. "I'm not sure I'm ready to be a dog owner. I think a puppy would be too much for me."

"We've always had goldens and they are the best dogs. I'm not sure I could handle not having one. If you travel often, it's tough because you have to find someone you trust to watch them, but I'm a homebody for the most part. This is the first time Willy and I have taken a trip on our own."

Norma noticed the flash of sadness in his eyes. "I remember the year after I lost Bob. That was the toughest. All the firsts without him. Anniversaries, birthdays, holidays—they were horrible. If it helps, it does get a bit easier with time."

He shrugged. "I sure hope so. I'm discovering I don't like living on my own, especially in such a big house. I just had my place assessed by a Realtor. I've been toying with the idea of putting it on the market. The girls are a little sad about it, but they understand. I'm also torn, but downsizing makes sense and a new start feels right to me."

"That's a big decision and not an easy one." She watched as Willy settled into the pillow and relaxed his head on the edge of it. "Are you getting hungry?" she asked.

He shrugged. "A little. I just went straight up to bed when I got home, so I missed breakfast and lunch. Neva forced one of her scones on me before I left, but I could eat."

She rose and said, "I'll fix us some plates and I've got some TV trays we can set up right here in the living room." She pointed to the corner, where a stand held the wooden tray tables. "You just relax and I'll be back in a jiffy."

In the kitchen, she retrieved her good dishes from the hutch and added a selection of leftovers to each of their plates. She toted out the napkins, cutlery, and glassware and put them on the trays Chet had placed in front of their chairs.

He insisted on helping her carry the plates and she grabbed the bottle of wine and some water. "Care for a bit of this with your water?" She held up the wine.

"I'm driving, so I probably better pass and stick to my water regiment." He poured the golden liquid into her glass.

The leftover picnic was just as tasty the second time around and they lingered, doing their best to clean their plates. Willy had closed his eyes long ago and was sleeping soundly.

As Chet poured another splash into Norma's glass, he gasped. "I almost forgot to tell you. When I was getting a coffee at Doc's yesterday morning, Calvin from the newspaper was in there. He said there's a little

Labor Day celebration going on this weekend in the town square. Sounds like they feature a few local bands. Anyway, one of the bands needs a guitarist. I guess their usual guy has to go out of town. I decided to stay and fill in."

Norma's heart beat a little faster. She'd have a few more days with Chet before what felt like her Cinderella moment was over. She hadn't let herself think about home for so long, but having him there, listening to what had become of his life, warmed her very soul. With the weight of their past firmly behind them, she was free to be herself again.

"What do you say, Norma?"

When she heard her name, she was jarred from her own thoughts. "Sorry, what was that?"

"I wasn't sure if you had plans already, but I was hoping you might be persuaded to join me at the celebration on Saturday. I think we only play for about thirty minutes, so it wouldn't be all evening with you sitting alone."

"Oh, that would be fun. The only thing I was planning to attend was the parade and pancake breakfast on Monday morning. This is the first year they've decided to add the music in the evening and I'd love to go."

He smiled. "Great, then it's a date." Panic filled his face and he added, "I mean not a date, per se…You know what I mean."

She laughed, almost choking on the wine she had just sipped. "I understand. Just two old friends spending time together. It will be fun." She'd thought she was the only one who was nervous and awkward, but Chet's red cheeks said otherwise.

Neither of them had room for dessert and Norma cleared the trays and returned a few minutes later with two mugs of tea.

While they sipped, they lamented the lack of television programming they enjoyed. Norma reached for the remote. "You know, I've started watching several British shows that I stream. I've been saving one called *New Tricks*, about a group of retired detectives who come back to solve cold cases in London. Would you like to try it?"

"Sure, the title is intriguing. Old dogs, new tricks, right?"

She pressed several buttons on the remote and started the first episode.

They laughed together at the quirky characters and the younger woman who oversaw their unit. After two cups of tea and two episodes, they took a break for cobbler.

Chet took his first bite. "Ah, this is delicious, Norma. I take it you enjoy baking?"

"I do like to bake. I'm not very artistic or creative with crafts, but baking gives me the satisfaction of making something myself. I don't do as much as I used to, since I'll end up eating it all. I usually just make something for the Winey Widows or community events. They're doing a bake sale for Labor Day, so I'll contribute something."

He licked his fork clean. "I'd say you have quite a talent. Between you and Neva, I'm liable to go home ten pounds heavier than when I left if I keep this up."

She nodded. "I know, it's hard to keep the weight off when we age, isn't it? I like to walk, so that's my main exercise. I try to get in a couple of miles each morning, until it gets too snowy."

He chuckled. "Winters are tough. My girls tell me I should join the gym so I have a place to exercise when the weather is bad. I'm just not much for that idea. I like the outdoors."

"I was considering joining ours. Everybody speaks highly of Pam, one of the trainers. She's a lovely young woman and I know her mother. I need to make more of an effort, because it's easy to just hibernate indoors when the snow flies. I like to knit and crochet, so I lead a little group down at the bookstore during the winter. It's a good incentive to get out of the house."

They talked about how their weather was very similar with lots of snow in January, especially, and the days upon days of below-freezing temperatures that made them hunker down at home with a fire. Chet set his mug on the coaster. "I've been giving Florida more thought these days. I'm not getting any younger. Yesterday was a good reminder of that."

"Jean, one of my friends, goes to Florida each winter. I always think that sounds divine and am a teensy bit jealous when she talks about it. Just think; no shoveling, no frozen toes or fingers. It sounds wonderful. It would be lovely to have a view of the water, live near the beach, even have a pool. I can imagine a sunroom for reading and watching the sunrise."

"That does sound inviting. I'm not sure I could give up our gorgeous autumns or enjoy Christmas without the mountains and snow, plus all the huge trees around this part of the country. I feel conflicted." He chuckled.

His grin faded. "I used to think we had all the time in the world to consider Florida. Now..." He shook his head.

"Don't rush. Take your time." Norma took a sip from her mug. "Grief does awful things to your mind. It's hard to figure out." She drummed her fingers on the edge of her mug. "You don't want to make a decision you'll regret later or pass up something that would be perfect. Maybe you should visit the area and see what you think."

"You're right." He nodded and collected both of their empty plates, taking them into the kitchen.

When he returned, Willy was sitting up, alert, watching him for his next command. "Dinner was lovely, and your cobbler was the best I've ever had. Oh, and thanks for introducing me to some new television options. I'm going to check into that when I get home."

She stood and grinned. "That show has twelve seasons, so you'll be set for a few evenings. Plus, I have a ton more to share. I'll have to get your email so I can send you some suggestions." She took a notepad from the drawer of the table next to her and wrote down her phone number, along with her cell number and email.

"Oh, yes. When we were young, I never could have

imagined that emailing people would be considered old-fashioned. All my kids want to do is text and it drives me nuts." He took the notepad and tore off her page and then wrote down his information and handed it back to her.

She smiled and scanned the page. "I'm not much for texting either. It takes forever and then I always find a grammar or spelling mistake. I'd much rather use a keyboard. So much has changed over our lives, hasn't it?"

He bobbed his head as he stood and motioned Willy to come to him. "And not all of it for the better. I miss the good old days when we were kids."

She stood and bent to pet the top of Willy's head. "You were such a good boy tonight."

"Thanks for a wonderful evening. If you're not sick of us by now, we'll take you up on your offer to join you on your walk in the morning."

She walked him to the door. "I look forward to it. I'll pick you up at Neva's."

He stood in the open doorway and inched closer to her, gripping her in a tight hug. She kept hold of him longer than she expected. It was warm and comforting, and it felt good to be held for the first time in a very long time. The scent along his collar made her want to stay locked in his arms even longer.

CHAPTER 8

$\mathcal{T}$he next morning, Norma bounced out of bed earlier than normal. She hurried to the bathroom mirror to examine her hair. It had held up well and she would never again doubt the magic of her grandma's satin scarf.

Then it survived being shoved under her shower cap and only needed a touch-up with the curling iron in a few spots. There was no hope for makeup, but even without it, she noticed a bit of color in her cheeks and she saw a new sparkle in her eyes. It must be the good night's sleep she's gotten last night.

She threw on her jacket and her walking shoes and headed down the street. Willy and Chet were waiting for her on the steps of the inn. "Good morning," said Chet. "Neva made me promise to bring you back for tea and scones when we're done."

"Ah, it's hard to resist her scones but sort of defeats

our purpose in walking. Are you feeling good and okay to walk?"

"Fit as a fiddle. I slept great last night and drank enough water to fill that swimming hole we visited. I picked up a blood pressure monitor at the drugstore so I can keep an eye on it, and it's been fine."

"Okay, then. Let's go." She led the way to the blocks off Main Street and through the residential area of downtown. It was a lovely morning, but autumn was around the corner and the chill in the air served as a reminder.

It didn't take long to warm up, as they looped through the blocks, with Willy's happy tail wagging from side to side. The modest homes, most of them older, were well maintained with green grass and well-kept yards. Like Norma's cottage, none of the homes downtown were extravagant, though many were larger and more suitable for families.

A few larger and newer homes were farther out of town, where a field had been divided into a handful of plots for homes, but outside of that one neighborhood, Linden Falls hadn't changed much in the last five decades. It still didn't have a big-box store or chain stores of any kind. Norma liked that. It made her feel safe and comfortable.

In an effort to fill the gap the lack of stores created, places like Town Square Books, Duncan's Hardware, and even Fisher Drug Store branched out and stocked all sorts of products not normally on their shelves. With no chains or electronic stores, Chet was in need of a new cell phone charger and asked Norma where he might find one.

"Jed over at Duncan Hardware has a small section of them. He can order you one if he doesn't have the right one. He's Paige's brother and more importantly he's Bentley's human. Jed's dad started the hardware store here and now Jed runs it."

"Oh, yes, Neva told me he watched Willy while I was away. That's great news about the charger. I was afraid I was going to have to get one online and have it shipped to Neva's. I'm used to being able to get just about anything on a moment's notice. This place reminds me more of how we grew up in Stockbridge."

They made a detour to the hardware store, and as Norma had predicted, Jed had the right one in stock. When Willy came through the door, Bentley made a beeline for him. They pawed at each other, wanting to play. Both almost the same golden color, they could have been brothers.

Norma kept watch over Willy while Chet paid for it and had Jed cut open the plastic container so Chet could slip it into his pocket while they finished their exercise loop. Chet had to tug on Willy to get him to leave Bentley and promised they'd come back soon for another playdate.

As they walked, Chet told her more about Concord, which was a thriving metropolis of almost fifty thousand people compared to Linden Falls and its small numbers. "Concord's experienced substantial growth since I first moved there, but it was never this pristine and small."

"The folks in charge here are committed to keeping Linden Falls the same. I think if you don't have all the shopping and conveniences, you have a better chance of keeping growth down. Most of the people looking to move from the cities think this is a step too far. They like their big stores and fast food, and we can't offer either."

He gazed down Main Street as they turned the corner. "I can see that. It's fun to visit and feels like a step back in time, but not everybody could deal with it."

"Right, our population is around three thousand, but if you're here from the middle of September through October, it doubles with all the tourists. It's crazy."

"Oh, yes, the leaf peepers. You're in prime country for that experience, plus all the local artisans and food. That's probably when the stores take in most of their annual revenue."

"Right. They have to squirrel it away for the winter months when visitors are few and far between. Not many billionaires here, but everybody helps one another and it feels like one big family most of the time."

"We get our fair share of tourists for the leaf season in Concord, but it's not near as noticeable as it would be in a small place like this. Lots of people stay in rooms in Concord and take day trips around the area to take in the fall colors."

"There's a big fall festival here and we draw them in by the thousands for that. It's a bit overwhelming for everyone, but like you said, it fills the coffers for the winter, and it seems to work for the businesses here. They all offer their goods at fair prices. They can't compete with the big guys, and everyone here knows that. We all work together to support our local businesses all year."

Chet and Willy led the way to Neva's door. "I like that sense of community. That's what's missing in larger towns and cities."

He held the door and Neva greeted her with a friendly smile. "Oh, I'm so glad you're both here. Come in, come sit down, and I'll get you a pot of tea." She leaned close to Norma and whispered, "I love your new hair. You look beautiful."

Norma couldn't remember the last time anyone had used the word *beautiful* to describe her. Outside of her mom and dad, Bob had been the last one. After she left home, she had made it her mission to stay under the radar, blend in, fade away into the background. Since she and Chet had talked that night at the bookstore, it was different. She was different.

The dark veil she figuratively wore had been lifted. She was excited again and not worried about someone finding out about her past. In fact, she needed to explain things to Neva, Paige, and the Winey Widows. After making such a fuss about not knowing Chet, it didn't make much sense that she was spending every spare minute with him now.

She was surprised her phone hadn't rung yet, with Agnes or Cecilia wanting to know more. The grapevine in Linden Falls was more reliable and faster than any fiber optics line the techies could ever invent.

She'd see if she could get them all to meet for lunch this week or maybe even dinner tonight.

While Chet took Willy up to his room so the dog could take his nap and they could enjoy their tea, Norma whispered as much to Neva.

Neva looked sheepish. "Actually, Agnes called me to see if I knew what was going on. She said someone had seen you two together in his rental."

Norma laughed. Agnes was definitely the hub for their information network.

Neva pointed back at the kitchen. "I put on a big pot of soup today and Chet had a message from Brian that they want to get together tonight to rehearse their songs, so he'll be gone. I've already invited everyone over for dinner and you can tell us whatever it is you want to share."

As long as Norma had known Neva, she'd never understand how she seemed to know before anyone else what needed to be done and arrange things so they'd happen, almost like magic. She and the Wishing Tree had that trait in common.

"Well, that sounds perfect. What can I bring?"

"Absolutely nothing. The ladies have it covered and

are on pins and needles to hear what you have to tell them."

Chet came back downstairs and eyed the plate of scones on the table. "You spoil me, Neva."

She poured them each a cup of tea. "You two enjoy. I'll be in the back if you need me."

He reached for a scone. "Sorry I was gone so long. I hooked up my phone to charge and had to call Brian from the band. He wants to rehearse tonight, so that nixes my plan of asking you to join me for dinner."

She waved her hand at him. "Oh, I've got dinner plans already. I'm coming to Neva's with a few friends."

He smiled. "Well then, that worked out perfectly. Brian promised chili and cornbread along with the rehearsal. They've got a barn outside of town."

She explained the road to take and that Brian's place had a green tractor mailbox that he couldn't miss. "I'm sure you could leave Willy and we could keep an eye on him or he could hang out with Jed and Reed. They'll be in charge of Gladys."

"Oh, Willy would love that. Are you sure they wouldn't mind?"

"I can guarantee it."

He took a bite of the pumpkin scone with the maple glaze and groaned. "Oh, my, this is delicious. Between Neva's scones and all your friends, I'm going to miss this place."

She swallowed a sip of tea and thought he wasn't the only one that would be missing something.

CHAPTER 9

*O*n her way to Neva's for dinner, Norma made a point of walking down the street to check at Vera's shop. Her only client was coming through the door, saying goodbye to her. Norma took advantage of the empty shop and popped her head through the open door.

"Hey, Vera, I was hoping you might have time to show me some of the makeup you used on me. I'd like to get some supplies."

With a dramatic flourish, Vera brought her hand to her chest. "Miracles do exist." She rushed over to Norma and grabbed her hand. "Get in here."

Vera rifled through boxes and bins under the counter and came up with several small boxes. "This is the foundation I used. You don't need much; it just evens out your skin." She set another box in front of her. "Use this for blush, just a hint." She slid over two skinny boxes. "Mascara and lipstick." She bent down again. "Oh, and this is on me. It's a sampler of eye shadows in case you get brave, and here's a packet of makeup brushes."

She rang it all up and put it in a bag. "If you run into trouble, just call me."

Norma thanked her and stuffed the bag into her purse. "I love my hair, by the way."

"I'm so pleased. I'll put you down to come in next month for a touch-up." She pointed at a day on the calendar. "Just come at the same time."

She wished Vera a good night and hurried back to Neva's. She heard the women chattering long before she walked into the kitchen. When she came through the doorway they all quieted and looked at her, wide smiles on all their faces, wineglasses in their hands.

Agnes thrust a glass of wine toward her and Jean took her arm and led her to the table. Four sets of wide eyes stared back at her, willing her to spill it.

Norma took a deep breath and said, "First, I need to apologize for being untruthful with all of you. I do know Chet. We grew up together in Stockbridge."

Everyone except Neva looked shocked. Neva only smiled and gave a small nod to Norma, as if to encourage her.

She started at the beginning and told them about their scholarships and Chet's dreams of pro baseball. She described the accident and watched as Agnes and Cecilia clutched their hands to their chests.

Norma steadied her voice as she explained never going back to Stockbridge and disappearing at the small college in Vermont. She had to take a swallow or two of wine to make it through the part about missing her parents.

With the hardest part behind her, she smiled and relayed the story of Chet's life and how he had become a teacher and coach along with inventing a pitching machine. Her friends' eyes got even wider.

"Chet came here on a lark, filling in at the last minute for the drummer and at the urging of his friend Joe, who graduated from high school in Linden Falls." She smiled and shrugged. "Chet said it was fate and that it brought us back together again."

Norma cleared her throat and added, "I'm sorry I didn't tell you sooner. I was too ashamed to share my past and lived with such guilt over Chet for so long, I just wanted to forget about it and leave it in the past."

Cecilia reached for Norma's arm and patted it. "Don't give it another thought, dear. I'm just so happy Chet found you and set your mind at ease. It breaks my heart that you've been living with this for all these years and haven't been able to tell anyone."

The sting of tears threatened to dry up Norma's voice. She smiled at her oldest friend and nodded her thanks.

More wine was poured and the women peppered Norma with questions, soaking up the drama. Agnes threw up her hands and said, "This is just like one of those movies I like to watch and it doesn't hurt that Chet is such a handsome devil. He reminds me of Tom Selleck."

Norma stifled a giggle as she had been trying to figure out who Chet reminded her of and Agnes was spot on. The conversation quickly turned to the best-looking actors in their age bracket.

Neva dished up bowls of hearty potato and cheese soup while Jean sliced up the fresh bread she had picked up at the bakery. Cecilia retrieved a salad she had brought from the Crooked Porch, along with a bottle of their delicious house dressing.

Somehow, between all the questions and circular conversations, they managed to eat Neva's delicious soup. When the wine bottles were empty and they couldn't eat another bite, everyone left for their homes, with Norma volunteering to stay and help Neva clean up the kitchen.

Neva poured some of the leftover soup in a container and bagged up a few of her scones. "You take this home with you. That will save you making dinner one day this week."

"Aww, that's kind of you. Thanks. Thank you for hosting all of us tonight. I feel better having explained everything."

Neva smiled and gripped her shoulders. "You could have told me that story long ago and I wouldn't have judged you or thought any less of you. I always knew there was more to you than meets the eye."

Norma sighed. "I'm just glad I don't have it weighing on me any longer and seeing Chet again has been…well, special."

"And a bit exciting," said Neva, with a wink. "Take it

from me, I never expected to be romanced. At my age? It's a laughable thought, but there's nothing like an old flame and new love making your heart full again."

Norma nodded. Neva was right. There was something remarkable about rekindling an old relationship. The trust and familiarity were there, so it made things a bit easier, and at their age, time was of the essence.

Neva walked Norma to the door and then pointed at a box near the entryway. "I forgot, I've been cleaning out and going through old stuff, getting things ready for the thrift shop, and set aside some things I think might work for you. Take them and try them, and if not, just pass them along."

Norma couldn't get by Neva without a hug and thanked her again for the leftovers and the clothes on her way out the door. She stowed her packages in her car and was home within minutes.

She put the soup in the fridge and took the box into her bedroom, anxious to see what Neva had found for her. Her eyes lit up when she unearthed a beautiful sheer jacket in shades of teal and blue and a matching drapey shell for underneath. Next came a pair of soft slacks in dark blue that went with both pieces perfectly.

The last time Norma had been this excited about clothes was when she found a pair of insulated winter boots when Cecilia dragged her to the thrift store on one of her bargain-hunting trips. This, though, was not just functional, this was a gorgeous new outfit.

The box held more practical items that looked like

they could have come from Norma's own closet. Sturdy turtlenecks in colors she didn't have, a couple of cardigans that were shorter in length, a crisp white blouse with tasteful floral embroidery across the chest, some jeans and twill trousers, even some brand-new socks spilled out of the box. Between Cecilia's thrift shop finds she always shared and Neva's generosity, she'd have a whole new wardrobe.

She held the jacket up again in front of her mirror, checking her reflection. She couldn't wait to try on all three pieces. She hoped the pants were long enough. With her height, she had a hard time finding the length she needed.

She stripped off her clothes and stepped into the new hand-me-downs, which looked like they'd never been worn. As soon as she slipped the pants on, she smiled. The hem went all the way to the floor. She studied herself in the mirror, turning to each side, and grinned. Neva was right. The outfit was perfect.

Norma wasn't much for dressing up and didn't have many places to go. Her idea of fancy was wearing her red turtleneck with her Christmas cardigan, adorned with snow and cardinals. Since Bob had passed, she went to Neva's for Christmas and usually Agnes and Cecilia joined her. She had worn that same cardinal sweater every year.

As she looked in her closet for a good pair of shoes, it occurred to her she might want to treat herself to a new outfit for this Christmas. It would need to be warm, of course, but maybe it was time she updated her holiday sweater.

The shoes she reserved for church, weddings, and funerals, which sadly was where she wore them most, worked with the pretty blue outfit. She took one more look and then changed into her pajamas, taking care to hang her new clothes and checking the labels to see if they needed handwashing.

She padded into the kitchen and started some tea brewing and then wandered into the living room and flicked on the television. Once her tea was ready, she snuggled under her favorite warm blanket and started another episode of *New Tricks*.

She caught herself turning to Chet's empty chair to comment on something funny. She should have told him to stop by after his rehearsal.

Norma reached for the leather journal next to her chair and turned to a new page. She had used it to write to Bob after he'd passed. It was a way to share her day with him, and although some might think it odd, it comforted Norma. With his death so sudden, she'd had a hard time in the early days and used the journal as a coping mechanism. Now, she simply enjoyed it and it was a way to feel connected to her husband.

Tonight's entry was a long one. As she wrote and explained she had been too ashamed to share the story of her accident and Chet's injuries, tears pooled in her eyes. She dabbed at them with a tissue and powered on to explain how his appearance in Linden Falls had forced her to confront what had happened and that it had actually been somewhat of a blessing. She finished it off, letting Bob know how nice it was to connect with Chet again and how much fun they'd had at the falls. She hadn't realized how much she had missed having such companionship.

She went to refill her cup and an odd noise made her stop pouring in midstream. She frowned, trying to figure out what the sound was, almost like wind chimes. It sounded like it was coming from the kitchen table. She stepped closer and spotted her handbag she had dumped there when she came home from Neva's.

She rifled through it and retrieved her cell phone. She saw a light flashing and tapped on the screen. She rarely used that darn thing and only kept it around for emergencies. She probably needed to charge it up soon.

She smiled as she saw a text from Chet. *Just thought I'd say good night. Didn't want to call in case it was too late. Just got back to the inn. I've got some business I need to take care of tomorrow, so I'll be tied up most of the day. How about dinner at the Crooked Porch at seven?*

She nodded as she read the message. She couldn't think of anything clever to say back to him. Another reason she hated texting. It was so hard to infer the tone or understand feelings. She finally tapped in: *I'd love it. I'll meet you there.*

Moments later she heard the wind chime noise again. *A gentleman always picks a lady up for dinner. I'll see you at your place. Sweet dreams, Norma.*

His reply made her laugh. Now, how could she end a text conversation? Should she reply and then he'd reply again? Another reason talking was better. She decided to use an emoji. She surmised they had been invented by someone who couldn't figure out how to end a conversation via text. She found a sleeping emoji and sent it.

She noticed the low-battery warning and dug the charger out of the drawer and plugged in the phone. Chet didn't respond, so the emoji must have done the trick.

She took her tea and went back into the living room, glad that Chet had taken the time to check on her tonight. It warmed something deep inside her to know he was thinking of her.

She settled back into her chair, happy she had a dinner plan with Chet for tomorrow night but, at the same time, disappointed that he and Willy wouldn't be joining her for her morning walk.

FRIDAY MORNING, Norma rolled out of bed later than usual and enjoyed a steaming mug of tea before she slid her feet into her walking shoes, determined to burn off some of the calories she had consumed last night. The bread had been so good she had eaten two thick slices, slathered with butter. Between that and the soup, she'd eaten enough carbs for two days.

She took the longest route and ended up at the town square close to nine o'clock. Paige was just opening the bookstore and Norma wandered through the door.

Paige looked up from the cash register. "Morning, Norma. I'm so glad you're here. I was going to call you later."

"I'm just on my walk, a little later than usual, and saw you were opening. Just stopped in to say hello, but what did you need?"

"I hate to ask this on such short notice, but would you mind watching the store for a few hours tomorrow afternoon?" I promised Reed we'd go pick apples out at the farm and tomorrow's the only day that works. We were going to stop for a bite to eat, so maybe from noon until about three o'clock? Four at the latest."

"Sure, I can be here. No problem at all. Chet's playing in the band, but not until five thirty, so that works great."

"Thanks, Norma. Gladys will be with Jed, so you won't have to worry about her. Well, unless she decides to wander back down here." Paige laughed.

"I admire her independence," said Norma, bending to give the sweet dog a quick pat on the head. Gladys was known for roaming around town and visiting all the shopkeepers as she went between the bookstore and the hardware store, where she liked to spend part of her day with Bentley.

After perusing the shelf with new books, Norma wished Paige a good day and resumed her walk. Across the square, Norma saw Neva, who was retying a wish that had come off the Wishing Tree.

Finished, she stepped from under the canopy of green leaves and her hair glinted in the morning sunlight as she admired the tree. Norma came up the sidewalk and hollered out, "Morning, Neva. Your tree looks lovely."

She turned, smiling. "I just finished restocking the ribbons and collected a few of the older wishes to make room for the weekend. With so much going on, I'm sure we'll have plenty of visitors."

"I wanted to thank you for the clothes. I just love that blue outfit with the pretty jacket and the pants fit perfectly. All the other pieces are wonderful, but that outfit is stunning. I just need a good excuse to dress up and wear it."

Neva's eyes, full of whimsy, sparkled. "I'm sure you'll find just the right occasion for it and am thrilled you like it." She gave the tree another once-over and then said, "Come and join me for a cup of tea. I've got a fresh batch of scones in the oven."

CHAPTER 10

*N*orma nattered away the entire morning visiting with Neva and was quite proud that she limited her scone intake to half of one. Part of her had hoped Chet might still be at the inn, but with a little prodding, Neva let her know he had left early in the morning, after dropping Willy at the hardware store.

As Norma started to walk home, she wondered what business Chet was attending to and where he had gone. It must be something to do with his pitching machine sales. After his trip to the hospital, she hoped he was feeling up to it. Worry tugged at her, thinking of him driving somewhere alone.

She took a deep breath and shrugged as she made her way down the sidewalk. She'd have to wait and ask him for the details at dinner tonight.

The red door at Town Square Books beckoned her.

She had been tempted by a new book she wanted to read when she saw it earlier and decided to splurge on it and spend the afternoon reading. Norma plucked a copy off the shelf and waited while Paige finished helping a customer in front of her.

Paige smiled at Norma and ran her hand over the cover. "I was surprised you didn't snatch this up when you were here this morning."

Norma grinned. "You know me so well. I decided to spend the afternoon reading, but I didn't bring my wallet, so I'll pay for it tomorrow if that's okay."

"Since you won't ever let me pay you when you watch over the store, consider it a gift." Paige was always more than generous with Norma, giving her a huge discount and often paying her in books when she helped at the store. Norma tried to resist and insist she pay, but arguing with Paige was futile.

Norma's smile widened. "You are too good to me. Thank you, dear. I'll be here tomorrow."

Norma scooted across the street and made a quick dash to the box under the Wishing Tree, where she plucked a fresh card with a ribbon and scribbled her wish on it. She hadn't hung a wish in her branches in too many years to remember but had been pondering it as she gazed at the tree from the bookstore's window.

If she thought about it too long, she'd chicken out. She tied her wish to a low branch, hoping nobody had paid her any attention. She clutched the book in her hand and quickened her pace, anxious to get home and escape between the pages.

>))⟩

FOUR HOURS LATER, Norma forced herself to close the book, leaving the last third or so for tomorrow. She had hoped it would last through the weekend, but she knew better. She could never make a new book last much longer than a day. She eyed her shelves filled with old friends that had been with her through the best and worst times of her life.

She had found such solace in books, especially when she had moved away from home. She'd always loved to read, but the library had been her refuge and it was when her plans changed. The hours she'd spent in the beautiful college library had shaped her desire to become a librarian.

She would always remember the kindness of the librarian, Mrs. Price. She felt safe there and the idea of spending her days surrounded by books, order, and quietness appealed to her.

Throughout her career, she hoped she had been the quiet comfort for others like Mrs. Price had been for her.

After Bob had passed away, she turned to her beloved books again, losing herself, giving her a place to go to escape the harsh reality that she was alone again.

It reminded her of being alone those first months at college in Vermont, but far worse. She had been able to phone her parents, write them letters, meet new friends, and look forward to graduating. Now, there was much more to look back on than there was to anticipate in the future.

Bob's sudden death had been a harsh blow. He'd been the one to lead their adventures, which were small but included a few trips to places nearby. He preferred to drive, so their travels were limited to the time they could be away from the business.

Along with vacations and day trips, their dreams of Florida had died with him. Norma had used up her courage to venture out on her own in her youth. She was content to stay in Linden Falls, surrounded by life-long friends and the community she had come to think of as her family.

It wasn't exciting, but it was safe, and after what she had been through in her early years, being alone was easier in a place she loved, with people who cared for her and whom she loved. Being part of the Winey Widows had been a true blessing in her life.

Their weekly get-togethers forced Norma out of the house and Margot's idea to have a knitting club eased the isolation and loneliness the winter months could bring.

Their little club had opened her small world and given her something to look forward to each year with their one big trip they planned. Norma would have never ventured out on her own, but being part of a group made it fun and safe. She was already looking forward to Vancouver Island.

She'd be lost without Neva and Cecilia, especially.

Although others might think Norma's life was small and dull, she was content.

After her shower, she spent time styling her hair like Vera had shown her, and after watching an online tutorial targeted at mature women, she added a touch of makeup. She chose the white blouse with black embroidery and the shorter black cardigan Neva had given her. The style reminded Norma of Margot. She hadn't been into high fashion but had a few classic pieces and always looked pulled together.

It had been years since she'd taken this much time getting ready. She always admired Jean's style, but Norma's practical nature viewed the time she wasted on fashion and makeup as frivolous and wasteful. She had lived at the other end of the spectrum for so long with the same clothes and no-nonsense style. Maybe she'd found a happy medium in her recent upgrades.

She felt more than a little foolish, but seeing Chet sparked something inside her, something she couldn't quite describe. It was reminiscent of those early days when she had first met Bob.

Excitement fluttered through her as she checked her hair one more time. She smiled at her reflection, loving her new style. It and the hint of color on her lips and cheeks really did shave away a few years.

She left the bathroom and went to collect her purse. Moments later, Chet knocked on the door. She checked the time and smiled. He was a few minutes early.

Chet greeted her with a hearty smile. Norma wasn't sure if it was his dimples or the blue eyes that took her back decades, but something about him weakened her knees.

"You look lovely," he said. "Are you ready to go?" He extended his arm to her.

She nodded and slipped her arm into his. "How was your day? Are you feeling okay? I was a bit worried about you."

"Fit as a fiddle," he said. "But I'm touched you were worried. I think the doc was right about the medication. I've felt better since he switched it." He opened her door and made sure she was settled.

Minutes later they were sitting at a corner table inside the Crooked Porch with a view of Main Street. Nicole took their orders and brought them a basket of freshly made bread laced with rosemary.

"So, you handled whatever business you needed?" Norma asked, hoping she didn't sound too nosy.

They each took a slice, and as Chet slathered butter across his, he said, "I think so. I ended up driving back to my place. My Realtor friend had somebody looking for a place just like mine and wanted to know if I wanted to sell."

He took a bite and then sighed. "I needed to talk to the girls and make sure they were okay with the idea. I mean, I sort of knew they'd be disappointed but wanted to see if I could make them understand."

She met his eyes, unable to tell if he had been successful.

He shrugged. "I was hoping to talk to them in person, but logistically, it wasn't going to work. I got them both on a video call." He chuckled, "When we were kids, who would have thought we'd have that ability?"

"Never. I'm not much for all the technology, but it's nice to see faces, since people tend to say much more with facial expressions."

He nodded. "Right. Like I said, they weren't thrilled, but they're also not the ones tasked with taking care of everything. They're not little girls anymore and they don't visit like they used to. They have a strong attachment to their family home, but in the end, they said they'd support my decision."

Nicole delivered their bowls of homemade soup. Tonight's was French onion and the browned cheese on top made Norma's mouth water. In between bites, they continued chatting.

"Does the Realtor think the prospective buyer is serious?" she asked.

"Serious as in he's offering cash and wants to move quickly."

Her eyes widened. "Wow, that's a big decision. Where will you go?"

"Nothing's definite yet, but I've got my Realtor checking into a few options." He took a sip from his water glass. "I need some time to have the girls come up and take whatever they want. Then I'll sell some of it and figure out what to keep. Get organized and all.

Nancy and I collected quite a bit of stuff over the years."

She noticed the sheen in his eyes. "I know how you feel. It's hard to go through all those memories." She cleared her throat. "If you'd like some help, I'm happy to lend a hand."

He smiled and reached across the table for her hand. "I'd love that."

Nicole arrived with their dinner plates and they dug into the herb-roasted chicken and veggies. The tender chicken was melt-in-your-mouth good and the veggies were fresh and tasty.

Norma sensed Chet needed to talk through the idea of selling his house and saw the uncertainty in his eyes when he mentioned his girls, Annie and Kristy. He was torn and didn't want to disappoint them.

They lingered over their meal, talking more than eating. "I know it's a shock for the girls, so I'm trying not to be too disappointed in their initial response. As we talked, it got better. I just know it's not what they were hoping."

"Not having children, I'm the last one that will pretend to know how to handle that issue. I think you're doing the right thing by explaining it to them. They're old enough to understand the work involved in taking care of a big house and property. But I also understand how grown children struggle with losing the tie to their family home. They have lots of memories and an idyllic life wrapped up in it."

He nodded. "Yep, I remember after Dad died, helping Mom with the sale of the ranch and how difficult that was. I understand how they feel, but it doesn't change reality. I even offered it to them. Told them I'd carry the papers on it."

"That was a good idea. Smart, too."

"Exactly. When they both said they didn't have time to take care of it or the money to hire someone to do it, I think they realized what I'm facing."

"Very savvy of you and drives home the point without beating them over the head."

"All those years in the classroom, negotiating with some difficult kids taught me you have to make your idea seem like their idea and then everything goes much smoother." He winked and Norma's heart fluttered.

He was still as charming as ever. "I used to envy folks who had big houses and acreages, but with all that comes lots of work and expense. I'm happy with my little cottage. I can take care of most things myself, although I do hire a young man to mow the grass for me."

He bobbed his head. "That's what appeals to me about downsizing. I don't need much, and I don't want to be anchored to a place that is going to take all my time and energy. I'm not getting any younger, and after losing Nancy, I've decided I want to do a few things."

He finished his last bite of chicken. "With their blessing, or at least their understanding, I told the

Realtor to go ahead and draw up the paperwork. The buyer is offering more than I was going to ask, so I think I need to strike while the iron is hot. The real estate bubble is bound to burst, and I might as well sell high if I'm selling."

"How much time will you have to get out?"

His jaw tightened. "That's the kicker. Nobody wants to move to this area in the winter, so I'm trying to stretch it to forty-five days, but they prefer thirty."

"Oh, that's quick. How long of a drive is it from here?"

"About ninety minutes."

She nodded. She didn't drive outside of town at night. Her vision wasn't what it used to be, so she'd have to schedule her trips to help to be home before dark.

He glanced at the dessert menu Nicole had left on the table. "If the sale goes through, which I'm sure it will, the girls will come up next weekend, with their families, and take what they want. I've got lots of great friends who can help me if I end up having to put anything into storage. I need to go through my barn. It's full of decades' worth of treasures." He gritted his teeth. "I'm dreading that."

He handed her the dessert offerings with a quizzical look. "I don't know about you, but I'd rather have a piece of your cobbler and maybe watch another episode or two of that show."

Her heart warmed. "That sounds perfect to me."

As they left the restaurant, he reached for her hand

and squeezed it. "Thanks for listening and your offer to help. You don't know how much that means to me."

She didn't trust her voice. She loved the feel of his hand in hers, the strength, the support. She loved being with him. How in the world was she going to cope when he left in just two days?

CHAPTER 11

$\mathcal{S}$aturday morning, Willy and Chet joined Norma on her walk. The town was bustling with activity, with town square already set up with chairs and a few tents offering snacks and food, and even a few crafters. It was nothing like the huge fall festival, as this event was designed for the locals, with only a few visitors making the trip to Linden Falls.

The golden rays of the sun blanketed downtown, promising a lovely day. The glittery ribbons twinkled as the sun hit them, making the Wishing Tree look magical. She wanted to believe the glint from one ribbon that caught her eye was a sign that her wish might be granted. Her practical side knew it was fanciful, but she couldn't deny the glimmer of hope.

They took their time strolling along Main Street, Norma soaking up the time with Chet, trying not to think about Monday morning, when he'd be heading back to New Hampshire after the parade and breakfast.

He stopped in front of the bakery and looked at her, his brows arched, as if waiting for a response. Willy wagged his tail.

Norma realized the last thing she remembered was Chet talking about going out to Brian's house to rehearse again. They had to be at the square by five o'clock but wanted to squeeze in more time to practice, so he'd be there while Norma was covering for Paige.

She'd been lost in her own thoughts, worrying about him leaving, and hadn't been paying attention. "I'm sorry, I was daydreaming."

"I just thought maybe we should stop in for a bite to eat, since we'll be busy at lunch. I've already got us dinner reservations for tonight after we play. At Bistro Claudine's."

"Oh, how exciting. I haven't been there but have heard wonderful things. It's a bit fancy, you know?"

"So I've been told." He grinned and led her into the bakery. They ordered a breakfast sandwich and took it to go, picking up lattes at Doc's and finding an outdoor table, to accommodate Willy and take in the fresh air.

As they ate the sandwich, made with their flaky croissants, Chet pointed across the street to the stage they had set up at town square. "We're set to play until six o'clock. I'll just come look for you as soon as we're done."

"I'll be in the front row, cheering you on. I already asked Neva to save me a seat, since I wasn't sure what time it would start filling up with spectators. Now, with our fancy dinner, I'll for sure need to go home and change, so I won't be there very early."

They finished their breakfast and Chet and Willy escorted Norma back to her cottage, with Chet holding on to her hand most of the way. He hugged her goodbye at her door. "I'll see you tonight."

She stood on her porch, watching as the two of them meandered down the road. A man and his dog. She couldn't ignore her feelings for both of them.

She had let far too many years go by and hidden from life for far too long because of what she thought had happened. Her stubbornness served her well in many areas but had failed her greatly in cutting off anything to do with Chet and her past. How she wished she could go back in time.

She had subjected herself to a lonely existence in her college years. Granted, she would never have come to Linden Falls and found a home she loved, a true community, and her sweet love, Bob.

The what-if game never ended well.

She had the life she was supposed to have. She believed that, but she could have been happier had she listened to her parents, who had begged her to come home. They had assured her things would be fine, but she hadn't believed them. She'd thought they were just trying to console her and the shame she felt had never faded. She couldn't face everyone back home. She had been a coward and had missed too much.

If only the lessons you could see so clearly with age

were learned in youth. Alas, that wasn't how things worked.

If only she hadn't squandered all those years and had kept in touch with Chet.

She needed to make the most of it now. At least she knew she'd be seeing him again after he left Linden Falls. She wasn't sure what she had been thinking offering to help him pack and move. At her age, it wasn't like she'd be much help lifting and carrying things.

For once, she hadn't thought much and just blurted it out. It was a way for her to stay connected and see him again. Blood rushed to her cheeks with the realization that he probably saw her offer for what it was—a bit of desperation.

He'd seemed happy enough about it, so maybe he wanted to see her again, too.

A young boy speeding past on his bicycle interrupted her thoughts. How long had she been standing on her porch? She checked her watch and hurried inside. Her mind was wandering more today than ever.

After a quick trip to the powder room, she grabbed her new book and her purse and drove to Town Square Books.

Paige waved as Norma came through the door. "Thanks again for helping out today. We appreciate it so much." She eyed the book in Norma's hand. "We haven't been very busy today. I think there are too many other fun things going on, so you should have plenty of time to read."

Norma laughed and took her place in a comfortable chair behind the counter. "You two enjoy yourselves and I'll see you later this afternoon."

Paige opened the door that led to the house. "We'll bring you back some apples and I just brewed you a fresh pot of tea. There's loads of stuff in the fridge if you get hungry."

Norma thanked her and waved goodbye. As she watched the two walk down the sidewalk, hand in hand, her eyes filled with tears. Margot would have been thrilled to see Paige happy again. She wished she had lived long enough to witness it.

She glanced at the tree, remembering Margot's steadfast belief in her tree. Norma had never been one to put all her faith in the Wishing Tree but had admired Margot's devotion to it and her unwavering trust, no matter that not all her wishes had been granted. She hoped a little bit of Margot's faith would rub off on her.

Over the next few hours, she sold a handful of items, drank two pots of tea, and was able to finish her new book. She closed the cover and sighed.

Along with the satisfaction that came with knowing how things worked out in the story came the despair of it ending. This happened with each new book she read. She could never pace herself to savor it.

Luckily, she had access to all the books in Paige's store, plus the local library. For as small as Linden Falls was, they had been blessed with a well-stocked library. Books and her knitting kept her going all winter long.

She'd been pondering Chet's idea about getting a dog. She was warming to it, and while the idea of a puppy intimidated her, the thought of having a connection to Chet through one of Willy's pups was tempting.

Town square was getting busier, as people arrived to watch the bands. Norma was watching from the front of the store when Paige and Reed came down the sidewalk, both of them toting bags.

She opened the door and they came through it, laughing. Paige held out a small paper bag. "We've got loads of apples, along with apple pies, and we brought you some of those yummy apple cider donuts as a thank you. Be sure and take some apples if you'd like some."

She couldn't resist popping one of the bite-sized donuts into her mouth. "Oh, those are delicious. Thank you. I need to get home and change, but save me enough apples to make a pie and I'll pop in and pick them up later. The Winey Widows would enjoy a pie next week."

"You got it," said Paige. "We'll see you later. We're going to come and listen to the bands, especially Chet's."

Norma collected her book and purse and made for the door. "See you there."

NORMA USED every minute of the next hour, fixing her hair and carefully applying a dusting of eye shadow and mascara. She slipped into the new outfit she had been dying to wear, thankful for the excuse of an elaborate dinner.

She fussed with the jacket until she was happy with how it hung, then dug into her jewelry box. She wore the only fancy earrings she owned—a pair of tiny diamond studs Bob had given her for their twenty-fifth anniversary. She tried on the few necklaces that hung along one side of the velvet box, but none of them looked right. She opted to forgo them all and stick with the earrings.

She slipped into her dress shoes and took one more look in the mirror. She almost didn't recognize the woman smiling back at her.

CHAPTER 12

*N*orma parked her car on the side of Town Square Books and hurried across the street. A band with a talented fiddler was playing as she made her way to the front row, where she had already spied Neva's silvery hair. She slipped into the chair next to her and whispered a hello to Henry on the other side of Neva.

They were so sweet together. Perfect for each other. They were an inspiration that love could be found at any age.

As Norma listened to the band, she craned her neck, hoping to see a glimpse of Chet, but makeshift screens set up on the sides of the stage blocked the view.

When the band played their last song, the crowd cheered them on and the announcer made his way to the stage. "Let's hear it for Pickin' and Grinnin', the gang from Arlington." Everyone gave them another round of applause as they collected their instruments and left the stage.

"Next up, we've got a great local band. Our own Aches and Pains will be entertaining us tonight and they've recruited a guitarist that some of you may recognize as the drummer from the Rockin' Chairs when they performed here at the all-class reunion. Give a big hand to Aches and Pains, with guest guitarist and vocalist Chet Nelson."

The band came on stage to the whoops and hollers of the crowd. They played several songs with Brian and Chet sharing the vocals. Norma had never heard him sing, but his voice gave her goose bumps.

The crowd sang along to old favorites, and then when Norma thought they were done, Chet stepped forward to the microphone.

"Thank you all for such a warm welcome. I have a song I'd like to sing tonight and this one is for a very special lady named Norma." He pointed at her and smiled. "She's sitting right there in the front row and I'm sure you all know her. We grew up together, and while we haven't seen each other in over fifty years, it feels like we've never been apart. Anyway, this one is for you, my dear."

Being the center of attention was something Norma avoided, but she kept her eyes focused on Chet and his reassuring smile.

The band started to play, including Chet on his guitar. The smooth notes from his guitar filled the air and his gravelly voice sang the first words. It took

Norma the first verse to recognize the song and then she heard the title in the lyrics, "Marry Me," and understood. She clutched her hand to her chest, tears brimming in her eyes.

She saw Chet nod at her as he sang.

She glanced over at Neva, whose eyes were shiny with tears of her own. Neva reached for her friend's hand.

Norma couldn't believe her ears or her eyes. This was the most romantic thing she could imagine. She never dreamed she would be serenaded with a proposal, but here she was in the middle of town with a handsome man doing just that. The townspeople of Linden Falls had never really noticed Norma much, but now all eyes were on her.

She listened as Chet asked her to marry him in the lyrics of the song. The relief and excitement that filled her outweighed any embarrassment at being the subject of such a public proposal.

Chet had made a risky move.

He must have been certain she'd say yes.

The song finished and Chet handed his guitar to Brian and came down the steps at the front of the stage and then knelt before Norma. "I hope you're not upset, but I wanted to make this a memorable moment."

She laughed, tears filling her eyes. "You succeeded."

He produced a velvet box from his jacket pocket, revealing a beautiful diamond ring. He got down on one knee. "I meant every word, Norma. I love you and I think I always have. Will you do me the honor of marrying me?"

She nodded, noticing the glint of her ribbon hanging in the Wishing Tree. "Yes, Chet, I will."

He stood, getting a helping hand from Henry, and took Norma's hand in his. He brought her to her feet and bent and planted a long kiss on her lips.

The crowd roared with applause. When he finally let her go, she heard the announcer say, "Well, folks, I'm not sure how our other competitors are going to top this one. Congratulations to Chet and our very own Norma. We're thrilled for both of you."

Chet put his arm around Norma's shoulders. "I've got one more little surprise for you." He took her hand, and together with Neva and Henry, they walked across the square to Neva's inn. Henry held the door as they stepped into the entryway.

Neva led the way through to the kitchen and out to the back porch.

When Norma looked out at the yard, she gasped. Beautiful lights had been strung all across the yard and in the trees. Round tables with white cloths were positioned across the grass, decorated with gorgeous hydrangeas and dahlias. Candles glowed in glass lanterns on each table and along the porch railing. All of her friends were standing there to greet her.

As she received hugs and well wishes from Cecilia, Agnes, and Jean, she found out they had all worked together, along with Reed and Paige, who asked a friend who went to the apple farm to drop off the goodies to assure Norma wouldn't be suspicious, to set up and decorate Neva's yard.

Paige hugged her close. "We hated lying to you but didn't want to take a chance you'd wander over to Neva's and ruin Chet's big surprise, so we had to keep you busy."

Happy tears leaked out of Norma's eyes. She couldn't believe everyone had kept such a secret and had created what could only be described as a fairy-tale setting. For her! Just plain old Norma!

Bistro Claudine's was catering the event and the servers were ready for everyone to take their seats. Neva's niece, Janie, was working with the girls near the porch, setting up a dessert table piled high with treats. Norma hoped that some of it was made by the so-talented Carly.

The Aches and Pains band played softly while the waitstaff brought out the first course. The food was lovely and delicious, but Norma's attention was focused on the people surrounding her, wishing her and Chet happiness.

She couldn't contain the tears as the people she'd known all of her adult life and considered family hugged her and showered her with well wishes. Vera told her she looked beautiful as she wrapped her in a tight embrace. Nicole from the Crooked Porch was there, along with Woody, who had left his pizzeria long enough to extend his congratulations. Everyone from Cobblestone Bakery & Deli, her knitting friends, and the ladies from the library were on hand. Even Millie

King had taken a break from working on her new store and stopped by to congratulate her. Loretta engulfed her in a warm hug before making her way in the house with empty pitchers to refill.

Emotion filled Norma and settled in her throat, making it impossible to speak. She whispered her thanks to each and every person who was there. As the servers removed the last of the dinner plates, Brian spoke into the microphone and invited everyone to join in dancing to a special song Chet had selected.

Chet smiled at her and took her hand, leading her closer to where the band was set up in the corner of Neva's gorgeous yard with the portable dance floor.

A few other couples followed, including Pam and Steve from the gym, and their very own famous English chef turned Vermont farmer, Verity, who appeared to melt into the arms of her beau. Verity and Jack moved back and forth gently, her youth apparent in her graceful moves.

Norma hadn't danced in years. Her stomach flipped as she looked out at everyone watching, many of them with their cell-phone cameras poised and ready. Chet put his hand on her waist and took her hand in his as the soft notes of "The Broken Road" began to play.

Phil Steele, their local attorney, danced by with Mary May on his arm. They made a fitting couple, and Norma was glad to see Mary looking so happy. Norma would bet that the floral arrangements all around were of Mary's design. She would have to thank her.

But as the notes of the song spoke to her, Norma

closed her eyes, letting Chet lead her and shutting out everyone else. She focused on the words and the soothing melody. By the time the song ended, her head was resting against Chet's shoulder. He whispered, "The song says it all. I truly believe I was led back to you and I'm so grateful you said yes."

He brushed his lips against her cheek and sent a tingle through Norma, making her shiver. He chuckled and wrapped his arms around her tighter.

Chet kept Norma on the dance floor far longer than she'd planned. Nicole, who Norma had no idea was so talented, led the group in several fun line dances. Norma had never tried it before and, after more than a few dances, realized it was a great way to exercise. Maybe she could talk Nicole into doing some classes during the winter months and get the Winey Widows to recruit some students.

As they walked back to the table, they were stopped every few minutes, as friends offered handshakes and hugs to Chet, excited to meet the man from Norma's childhood who had succeeded in capturing her heart.

Neva appeared at her side and ushered both of them to a long table set up near the porch steps. Norma's eyes widened at the spread before her. Beautifully frosted cupcakes that looked like hydrangeas, dipped strawberries decorated to look like tuxedos, cookies with her name and Chet's name, brownies, mini fruit cheesecakes, and stacks of pastel macarons were displayed among gorgeous flowers and candles.

Along with all the individual desserts, a beautiful

white cake decorated with glittery sugar and gorgeous white peonies took center stage. Norma marveled at the display. Everyone at the bakery and bistro must have worked all night to put it together.

Agnes and Cecilia made it their mission to keep the wineglasses full, taking bottles from table to table, while the waitstaff poured hot coffee and tea and encouraged the guests to select their own favorites from the dessert bar. Neva and Henry made sure and collected one of everything to bring back to the table they shared with Chet and Norma.

Calvin from the newspaper was on hand snapping pictures and talked the newly engaged couple into posing for several photos. He scribbled on his notepad as he asked them questions. Neither of them divulged the entire story of their youth, and just knowing that they had grown up together and drifted apart but found each other fifty years later was enough to satisfy Calvin, who couldn't wait to write an article and promised they'd be on the front page.

They made their way back to their table when Chet was intercepted by Reed and Jed. Norma smiled as she watched the three of them laughing and talking. Chet had always fit in so easily, even when he was a teenager. His kindness and charm had remained, and it was as if he had lived in Linden Falls all his life.

As the sun set and dusk settled over Linden Falls, the evening sky darkened and made for an even more magical setting. The twinkle lights, the flickering candles, the soft music, and the love of old friends made for a perfect evening. As Norma took it all in, she pinched her arm to make sure she wasn't dreaming.

This was all for her.

As she moved her hand, her eye caught the glint of the diamond on her finger. She and Bob had worn simple wedding bands, but she was already in love with the vintage filagree band and the tasteful diamond Chet had chosen for her.

She shook her head in disbelief. In a week, she had gone from hoping Chet wouldn't recognize her to accepting his proposal. It had been fast but, at the same time, years in the making.

As the band played their last song, Chet and Norma made their way to the dance floor again. When the last note was played, Chet took the microphone from Brian and thanked everyone for coming and for helping him plan the proposal and the dinner.

He glanced down at Norma and squeezed her hand. "I'm just glad she said yes. I'm a very lucky man to have found love again and with the girl I always had a crush on since we were in elementary school. Thank you again for making this such a special evening and for all you did to give my bride-to-be, my love, a night to remember."

The guests clapped and cheered as Chet and Norma waved goodbye, stopping to hug Neva and Henry, who handed Norma a box of leftover goodies to take home, before escaping through the side gate and across the street.

Chet made sure Norma got to her car, waited for

her to slide behind the wheel and bent to leave her with one more sweet kiss. "I've got one more surprise for you, but it will have to wait until tomorrow. I need to pick up Willy. He's spending the evening with Gladys and Bentley at the hardware store."

"Just tell me," she said, laughing.

"You'll have to wait until morning. I'll be by early with breakfast. Sweet dreams, my love." He hurried back across the street, waving as he went.

CHAPTER 13

Sunday morning, Norma woke early. She brewed a cup of tea and indulged in one of the almost-too-beautiful-to-eat cupcakes from last night. Some of the fog of excitement had worn off from last night's proposal and party and Norma's practical nature was kicking in and her mind was in overdrive.

What were Chet's daughters going to think of all this? She hoped they wouldn't resent her or make it difficult for Chet. If they were having a hard time with him selling the family home, how would they react to him remarrying? She imagined he would move into her cottage with her, but would he be able to adjust after having such a large home?

The more she pondered, the more her stomach roiled. She couldn't finish the cupcake, so she wrapped it up for later. She'd gotten carried away last night and never once considered all these questions.

For once in her life, she had no concrete plan.

When Chet had surprised her with such a romantic gesture and proposal, she let her heart speak and hadn't given a moment's thought to the complications that would come with a marriage.

She took a shower with the hope she'd come up with a solution to all the problems she was beginning to recognize. Emerging without any breakthrough revelations, she got dressed and fixed her hair.

As she brewed another cup of tea, a knock on her door startled her from her thoughts. She welcomed Chet with a hug and Willy with a good scratching behind his ears. She noticed Chet was carrying a bulging plastic bag with a logo she recognized from one of the big electronic stores, along with a bag from the bakery.

He followed her into the kitchen and plopped both bags on the table. "I picked up a couple of those break-fast sandwiches."

She brought two plates and two mugs of tea to the table. "What's in the other bag?"

He wiggled his brows. "One of my surprises." As they nibbled on breakfast, Chet explained he had bought a tablet for her and a router so he could set up a wireless network, which would let her use the tablet for reading or browsing online.

She opened the box and looked over the instruction sheet. "Paige has one of these. I just didn't want the hassle of setting up the wireless."

He winked. "Now you don't have to deal with it. It's actually easy and I'll show you how to use the tablet. I brought mine." He unearthed the charger for her new tablet and connected it to let it charge.

As soon as he finished his breakfast, she showed him her computer, tucked into a corner of the spare bedroom. He unboxed the router and fiddled with the cables and then sat down in front of her screen and tapped the keys on the keyboard.

Within about fifteen minutes, he pronounced it ready to use.

Norma's eyes widened. "Well, that was easier than I thought it would be."

He used a sticky note from the stack on her desk and wrote down the wireless password. "Okay, let's go back in the kitchen."

She refilled their mugs and joined him at the table. She sat next to him as he explained what he was doing on his tablet. "I bought you the same model, to make it easy."

Once he connected to the wireless, he showed her how the touch screen worked and the basic operations. "Now, here's the rest of my surprise."

He tapped the screen and a photo filled it. "Oh, that's a lovely view," she said, eyeing the water and palm trees.

He turned to her and smiled. His dimples were truly irresistible.

"Remember when we were talking about Florida the other day?" She nodded. "Well, I had my Realtor looking for a place there and he found the perfect one."

He flicked through the dozens of photos, showing

Norma the house with a view of the bay in a golf community in Destin. He smiled and pointed at the screen. "You said how nice it would be to have a sunny room to read."

Norma's eyes widened at the gorgeous outdoor living space within the screened patio, a pool, and a hot tub. The patio alone was bigger than her cottage. He kept scrolling and revealed the living space, an open design with a beautiful kitchen, wood and tile floors, two bedrooms, and an office.

She was speechless. It was beyond her wildest dreams.

"Do you like it?" Chet's forehead creased with concern.

"It's…it's marvelous." She used her finger and scrolled back a few photos.

"It's got all the things you mentioned, plus it's on the golf course, so I could play anytime I wanted."

She reached for his hand. "It looks perfect. I woke up this morning wondering if we got ahead of ourselves. What about Annie and Kristy? How are they going to handle this?"

He nodded and squeezed her hand. "That was what I was really talking to them about when I went home. We'd already had the conversation about selling the house, but I told them about you and my intentions."

She sucked in a breath.

He smiled. "I'm not going to lie and say they weren't shocked, but after we talked and I explained we grew up together and about the accident and how you had shouldered the guilt and responsibility for it all these years, worried that my life had been ruined, when in reality, my life couldn't have been better. They want me to be happy and they want to meet you."

"I'd like that. I just don't want to be the source of pain for them or for you. We both got swept up in the excitement and I can't be responsible for coming between you and your family."

He turned and wrapped her in his arms. "That's not going to happen. Trust me, Norma. They'll love you, just like I do. They know you're not replacing their mom and they both told me they could tell I was finally happy. They had been worrying about me, being without Nancy."

She relaxed as she let his words sink in and buried her head in his neck, inhaling the inviting scent of sandalwood and something tropical that washed over her. She shut her eyes and imagined Florida might smell just like him.

He released her but kept hold of her hand. "So, my idea was to live here in Linden Falls in your cottage for part of the year. We could spend summer and fall here. I'm sure the girls would like it if we spent Christmas here or with them and then we could hit the road for Florida and spend the worst part of Vermont's winters enjoying the sunshine and that view. We could also spend Christmas in Florida, whatever works." He poked the screen.

He met her eyes. "But that's just my idea. I want you

to be happy and comfortable. Tell me, what do you think?"

"I think it sounds wonderful. So much so, it's hard to imagine." She looked at the screen again. "Like we talked about, I'm not sure it would seem like Christmas without the trees and snow. Maybe at least this first year, we could wait until after the holidays to go." She grinned. "I admit, I'd love to see it in person though."

"That's a great idea. We could take a trip down there soon, before we have to worry about the weather. Leave a vehicle in the garage. I've got a battery tender we can hook up to keep the battery healthy. The HOA takes care of the yard maintenance and all that, and the house has an alarm and camera system, so we can monitor it from here."

He went on to explain with the community being popular with snowbirds, they offered several packages where staff members periodically could come in the house and check on things and check in with updates, plus take care of any issues. "The Realtor said we could also rent it out while we're up here, but I'm not wild about having strangers in my house." He let go of her hand and took a sip of tea.

She nodded. "I agree. That would make me uneasy." She pointed at the screen with the asking price, which was more money than she ever imagined spending. "That's a pretty scary number." She went on to explain she lived on her retirement pension so couldn't offer much financially.

He chuckled. "Your money is not important to me

and we'll see a lawyer and work out all the details so that if something happens to either of us, it's clear how our property will be handled. I don't want you to have to worry about the future. I have plenty of money, and with the sale of my house in New Hampshire, my accountant tells me buying the place in Florida is a good move tax-wise. The royalties I get from my pitching machine are enough to keep us more than comfortable for the rest of our lives and, long after I'm gone, will continue to go to my family.

Her shoulders relaxed. "I don't want your girls thinking I'm a gold digger or that I would take advantage of you in any way."

"Don't worry a moment about that. They know you weren't the one seeking me out. I called them late last night when I got back to the inn and told them you said yes and they're both excited to meet you. Like I said, our initial conversation was a bit rocky, and I understand it's a big change, like selling the house, but they noticed the change in my mood and want me to do what is best. They both agreed Nancy wouldn't want me sad and alone. They love the fact that we grew up together and have known each other so long."

She rewarded him with a smile. "Well, after last night, you know my friends here, who are my family, love you. As I watched you laughing with so many of them, in your easy way, I thought it seemed liked you'd lived here all your life."

"You've got some great friends and neighbors here.

I love it and how welcoming they've been to me. And I know my girls are going to love you."

He pointed at the tablet charging. "That's the other reason I wanted you to have the tablet. You can use the camera and we can do a video call with the girls so you can meet them."

She put her hand on his knee. "It's just been so fast. I'm not usually so spontaneous."

He patted her hand. "When Henry was driving me to the hospital, I decided right then and there, if I survived and was okay, I was going to marry you, Norma. I'm done wasting time. Losing Nancy taught me a harsh lesson. We thought we had time to do the things we wanted. Instead of waiting for the right moment or to finish whatever tasks we thought were so important, we should have jumped in with both feet. I'm not going to let that happen again. So, I made a promise to myself to embrace what I want to do and do it, without waiting for the right time. Starting with marrying you."

Tears burned the back of her throat. "I'm so glad you came to the reunion and stuck around."

He bent and kissed her. "I guess we'll have to invite Joe to the wedding, huh?"

The thought of a wedding and all it entailed made her stomach lurch. "How would you feel about something simple? Like going to the courthouse. I don't want a big to-do."

He let out a sigh and laughed. "You're in charge of the wedding. Whatever you want, but I'm relieved to hear you say that. I told the girls we'd come visit them after we were married, hoping you might be leaning toward a simple ceremony. I'll happily march down to the courthouse today and marry you. To me, it's not about the wedding, it's about our life together and how we make the most of it."

Norma had forgotten what it was to trust someone, depend on someone, and to feel such happiness because of that someone. Now Chet was her someone, and while their road had been long and winding, he was here now and had chosen her.

*N*eva insisted the two newlyweds come back to the Wishing Tree Inn for tea and scones before they hit the road for New Hampshire to get Chet's house ready to sell. Neva and Henry had served as witnesses in the judge's chambers where they were married and Neva had taken dozens of photos of the bride and groom and had the clerk take a few of the four of them together. On the way back from the courthouse, she asked to take their photo under the Wishing Tree.

Norma stood, in a beautiful pale blue dress that Jean had loaned her, next to her handsome husband, who wore a dark blue suit that matched his eyes. Neva took several photos and showed them her favorite, with Norma glancing up and Chet gazing down, both of them smiling, as if they shared a secret.

Neva grinned and linked her arm in Norma's as they walked across the square. "I'll get these printed and send them to you. I love seeing you so happy, my dear friend."

She led them into her parlor, where the table was set and waiting for them. As they settled into their chairs, Neva returned with a pot of hot tea, along with two wishes that hung from glittery ribbons.

She set the pot down and asked Henry to pour. She handed each of them a wish. "I wanted to give you these, since our old tree has seen fit to grant them."

Norma looked down at the wish, recognizing Chet's blocky print. *I'm tired of being lonely and wish for a second chance at love and happiness.*

She turned her head to look at the wish Chet was reading—her wish. *I wish Chet could stay with me forever. I don't want to be alone.*

They both smiled and linked hands atop the table. Chet shrugged. "Neva convinced me to tie a wish to that old tree the first day I was here."

Norma fingered the ribbon on her wish. "I haven't tied a wish to that tree since Bob and I were trying to have a baby. I guess your old tree really does have some magic left."

"Long overdue, I'd say." Neva lifted her teacup. "I knew there was a connection between the two of you the minute I saw you, Chet. I love it when hopes and wishes come true, especially for someone as dear to us as Norma."

They all raised their cups. "To many years of health and happiness," said Neva.

They clinked the rims of their cups together and

took a sip. "Maybe you two should think about making it official." Chet wiggled his eyebrows at Neva and Henry.

Norma smiled. "He's right. Life's short."

Neva pointed out the window. Norma gasped and said, "Oh, my, it looks like Vera's got trouble."

They stared as they watched Vera, her hair a startling shade of magenta, come out of the Post Office, which was now open for business, and shove a letter into her pocket. Her usual sunny and cheery disposition was underpinned with a new fretful air and stress showed around her downturned mouth. As ever when heartache hit, she went overboard with the bright colors, heavy makeup, and overt fashion as a distraction. Today, she was walking with more purpose and a new furrow to her brow as if worry was her constant companion.

Norma brought her hand to her chest and turned to Neva. "I'm concerned about her. I wonder if we should try and talk to her?"

Neva nodded. "Something's got her more than rattled. The poor girl's entitled to her privacy, but maybe I can figure out a way to help. Let me give it some thought."

To discover what has thrown Vera's world for a spin, read A WHOLE HEAP OF WISHES, the next book in the series by Amanda Prowse.

>>>>

★ Don't miss a Wishing Tree book! ★

BOOK 1 - *The Wishing Tree* a prologue book

Book 2 - *I Wish...* by Amanda Prowse

Book 3 - *Wish You Were Here* by Kay Bratt

Book 4 - *Wish Again* by Tammy L. Grace

Book 5 - *Workout Wishes and Valentine Kisses* by Barbara Hinske

Book 6 - *A Parade of Wishes* by Camille Di Maio

Book 7 - *Careful What You Wish* by Ashley Farley

Book 8 - *Gone Wishing* by Jessie Newton

Book 9 – *Wishful Thinking* by Kay Bratt

Book 10- *Overdue Wishes* by Tammy L. Grace

Book 11- *A Whole Heap of Wishes* by Amanda Prowse

Book 12- *Wishes of Home* by Barbara Hinske

Book 13- *Wishful Witness* by Tonya Kappes

We also invite you to join us in our My Book Friends group on Facebook. It's a great place to chat about all things bookish and learn more about our founding authors.

FROM THE AUTHOR

Thank you for reading the OVERDUE WISHES. I have a soft spot for librarians and more mature characters and enjoyed giving Norma her own story. I've also worked on my town's All-Class Reunion for years and enjoyed adding a bit of my hometown to Linden Falls. This has been a fun project, working with my author buddies from My Book Friends, and I hope you'll read all the books in the series. They are all wonderful stories centered around a special tree in Linden Falls. If you enjoyed this story, I hope you'll explore more of my work. You can find all my books on Amazon and many of them on other major retailers. The Winey Widows from WISH AGAIN and OVERDUE WISHES also feature in my GLASS BEACH COTTAGE SERIES, when they take a trip to the coast of Washington and spend some time at the cottage.

If you're a fan of mysteries, I write the COOPER HARRINGTON DETECTIVE NOVELS, a private detective series of whodunit murder mysteries. If you enjoy women's fiction, you'll want to try my best-selling HOMETOWN HARBOR SERIES, filled with stories of friendship and family, set in the islands of the Pacific Northwest.

The two books I've written as Casey Wilson, A DOG'S HOPE and A DOG'S CHANCE, both have received enthusiastic support from my readers and, if you're a dog lover, are must-reads.

If you enjoy holiday stories, be sure to check out my CHRISTMAS IN SILVER FALLS SERIES and HOME-TOWN CHRISTMAS SERIES. They are small-town Christmas stories of hope, friendship, and family. I'm also one of the authors of the best-selling SOUL SISTERS AT CEDAR MOUNTAIN LODGE SERIES, centered around a woman who opens her heart and home to four foster girls one Christmas.

I'm a huge dog lover and include dogs in all my books. I'd love to send you my exclusive interview with the canine companions in my Hometown Harbor Series as a thank-you for joining my exclusive group of readers. You can sign up for my newsletter at this link: https://wp.me/P9umIy-e

I hope you'll connect with me on social media. You can find me on Facebook, where I have a page and a special group for my readers, and follow me on Amazon and BookBub so you'll know when I have a new release or a deal. Be sure to download the free novella HOMETOWN HARBOR: THE BEGINNING.

It's a prequel to FINDING HOME that I know you'll enjoy.

If you did enjoy this book or any of my other books, I'd be grateful if you took a few minutes to leave a short review on Amazon, BookBub or Goodreads.

ABOUT THE AUTHOR

Tammy L. Grace is the *USA Today* best-selling and award-winning author of the Cooper Harrington Detective Novels, the best-selling Hometown Harbor Series, and the Glass Beach Cottage Series, along with several sweet Christmas novellas. Tammy also writes under the pen name of Casey Wilson for Bookouture and Grand Central Publishing. You'll find Tammy online at www.tammylgrace.com where you can join her mailing list and be part of her exclusive group of readers. She invites you to join her in My Book Friends, a fun Facebook group where readers and authors chat about all things bookish. Connect with Tammy on social media at the links below.

Made in United States
North Haven, CT
15 September 2022